AMANDA HEADLEE

MADNESS
and GREATNESS
can share the same face

MADNESS and GREATNESS

can share the same face

AMANDA HEADLEE

woodhall press

Woodhall Press | Norwalk, CT

woodhall press

Woodhall Press, Norwalk, CT 06855
WoodhallPress.com
Copyright © 2024 Amanda Headlee

Cover design: LJ Mucci
Layout artist: LJ Mucci

Library of Congress Cataloging-in-Publication Data available

ISBN 978-1-960456-25-0   (paper: alk paper)
ISBN 978-1-960456-26-7   (electronic)

First Edition
Distributed by Independent Publishers Group
(800) 888-4741

Printed in the United States of America

This is a work of fiction. Names, characters, business, events and incidents are the products of the author's imagination. Any resemblance to actual persons, living or dead, or actual events is purely coincidental.

Also by Amanda Headlee

Till We Become Monsters

Short Story Reprints

"The Journal of Milton Parker"
First published in *Consumed: Tales Inspired by the Wendigo*.
Denver Horror Collective, 2020.

"We Still Have Time"
First published in *Midnight from Beyond the Stars*.
Silver Shamrock Press, 2021.

"Where the Elk Roam"
First published in *That Darkened Doorstep*.
Hellbender Books, 2022.

For Andrea

Table of Contents

The Journal of Milton Parker

A prequel to *Till We Become Monsters*

The following are excerpts from the journal of Professor Milton Parker, professor of Biological Sciences at the University of Minnesota.

November 25, 1923

This morning, after skipping church service, Professor Marco Georges and I set off on a research expedition sponsored by the university to establish if a mountain lion population still existed in the forests of Grand Portage, Minnesota. We hired four locals who knew the forest well to accompany us as our navigators and protectors. Paul Warren, Timothy Matthews, James Pinkerton, and a man who just went by the name Michael were all hunters who spent their lives in the area. If Georges and I were the brains of this party, then Warren, Matthews, Michael, and Pinkerton would be the brawn.

We brought enough warm gear to last us the two weeks of the expedition. However, I am concerned about the food stores. A little after eight in the evening, after Georges and I settled into our shared rented room at the house just outside of town, Warren stopped by for an unexpected (and quite strange) visit. He had stopped by to discuss the amount of food the team would carry on the trip, saying only a week's worth of rations was needed. The extra weight was not worth hauling and would slow the group down. He and his boys would supplement the other week's rations by hunting game. He assured me we would not run out of food. I discussed the cons of that decision with him, but Warren said if I wanted to bring the extra food, I had to carry it myself; his men would not. I despise the gamy taste of wildlife, but Georges and I could not bear the additional weight split only between the two of us. Warren's preposterous idea left us with no other option. This morning, we begrudgingly left rations we couldn't carry with the owner of our rented room.

The easy trek through the forest brought Georges and me delight. Despite the cold and snow, beauty emanated from the deep woods with a sparkling, pristine effect. A few inches of snow on the ground did not slow us and was a godsend for tracking, or at least for Gorges and me.

Georges and I relinquished control of the search to the hunters, as tracking animals was pitched to us as their area of expertise. Truth be told, it is an area that I noticed only one of our hired men had a sense of skill at. Warren initiated the search by having us follow a game trail, saying that the best way to find a big cat was to follow the trail of what they eat. While Michael paid particular attention to our surroundings—he said he was looking for paw prints, bits of fur caught on a branch, or any other telltale sign of a big cat—the other three seemed oblivious to our surroundings. Warren kept a straight path along the trail, barely looking at the ground. Pinkerton and Matthews talked the whole time. Michael trailed behind the group and observed the land with a keen eye, though, despite his best efforts, he found no trace of the elusive mountain lions today.

A fury began to burn in me, because what was the point of paying for four hunters when only one of them was helping us in our search?

After nearly ten exhausting hours of hiking, we pitched our tents in a clearing under the stars, surrounded by large conifers that walled us off from the rest of the world as if we were tucked inside a fortress. The only sound heard was soft clumps of snow falling from tree limbs.

As I write this, Georges sits beside me, the need for rest written on his face. I am sure mine looks similar. My anger from the search earlier did not diminish, and I relayed my feelings to Georges as the hunters set up camp. He told me to let the anger go. It would do us no good on the trip and probably cause us some issues with Warren, Pinkerton, and Matthews if I confronted them. I won't say a word about my concerns with that crew, but I can't let go of my irritation with them. Especially sitting here and watching Warren, Pinkerton, and Matthews cajoling in splendor around a roaring fire as if they had had a successful day.

———

November 26, 1923

The trek started early, before the sun rose. After a quick breakfast of cured meat, bland hardtack, and coffee, we packed up and moved along. Warren led us deeper into the forest. The hunters walked with their rifles held in their hands, ready to fire at will. Matthews and Pinkerton flanked Georges and me. Michael took up the rear. Concern ate at my nerves as to why the hunters displayed such a defensive nature, since yesterday, Warren, Matthews, and Pinkerton had been having a good old time.

I asked Michael if the sudden defensive nature was because we were in mountain lion territory. Or was it something else? The only other carnivores in the forests to be wary of were wolves or a lone bear; however, Michael assured us that the bears would be hibernating and the wolves feared man too much to attack a group. I asked him how he could be sure of these assurances. As he walked, he gave me a sideways glance and said nothing. I do not know how to take that response and may press for more answers later.

———

Another fruitless day without a single paw print or bit of fur from a mountain lion being found. Georges's concern about the cats being extinct from this land may be valid. I believe humans are disrupting the ecological balance of the natural world, but I do not fully agree that we have made the creatures extinct in these parts. President Roosevelt endowed the United States with over two hundred million acres of protected landscape for wildlife conservation. Yet we see across the country that populations of various species are decreasing. I pray Georges's concerns about the cats' demise in this area were wrong. We are both quite passionate about animal conservation, to the point where Georges's wife joked that he loves animals more than her. A farce, for sure, as Georges doesn't love anyone or anything more in this world than his wife. Yet he and I are gravely concerned about the environment's future. Truth be told, being the most intelligent species on Earth makes us its caretakers, and we are all doing a poor job of caring for the planet.

After we pitched camp in another clearing, Michael and Pinkerton returned with a few rabbits. They were lucky to have found them, as they came across no other traces of wildlife. Michael had words about the lack of game with Warren, who dismissed him with a wave. The animals would appear under the warmth of the sun tomorrow. That statement seemed to bring Georges, Pinkerton, and Matthews comfort. Michael looked unnerved, and his worry increased my fears.

I am intrigued by Michael. His mother is from an Ojibwe tribe. His father is from New York by way of England, though he died when Michael was just a baby. I wanted to know more about his heritage but felt it best to ask him away from this crew. He may be more open to talking about himself if it were just me. The other three hunters seem to be good friends. Michael does not seem to be fully part of that crowd despite being recommended by Warren. He tends to sit outside the group and rarely speaks to the other hunters—or is spoken to by them. Aside from Michael, something about this lot makes me uneasy. Because of that, I don't trust them. I try to keep close to Michael as we trek. My instincts know he is a good person and an expert in this forest.

———

November 27, 1923

My and Georges's feet were infested with blisters from the snow wetting through our leather boots. Letting Georges handle water-proofing our boots had been a poor idea on my part, as he did not do a thorough enough job. We attempted to hang our socks to dry by the fire, hoping they would not be damp in the morning.

We trekked through the forest for three days with nary a sign of mountain lions or game beyond the rabbits from last night. At this point, we had eaten over a quarter of our rations, since Warren had forbade us to bring more. Georges suggested we return to restock, but Warren said it wasn't necessary. They would find game deeper in the forest to replenish our stores. I asked the men to watch how much they consumed until we found game. Warren laughed and told me not to worry. I fear he sorely miscalculated the availability of wildlife in this area. Luckily, with the abundance of snow, we did not require water, as we could melt snow into water after establishing camp.

I will not bring up the risk of running out of food again today, but it needs to be addressed soon. Georges and I agree that we must cut this trip short, as we cannot continue hoping that we will come across game. The hunters will not like the mandate, as they will only be paid for the days we are on the expedition. I shall wait to see tomorrow's progress before I say anything.

———

November 28, 1923

Today proved to be another failed day of finding evidence of our big cats. And the weather felt like it had a chill that made us believe it may take a turn. We cut the search short and established a new camp at around one in the afternoon.

With the tents pitched, the other three left camp to hunt our elusive dinner. The hunters dismissed my request to ration the food, and we ran out of the cured meats at breakfast this morning. Now we have resorted to rationing the johnnycakes and hardtack. Hardly nutritious, given the amount of hiking we had done. At least abundance still flowed with water and coffee.

After Georges excused himself to his tent for a nap, I spoke to Michael privately about his culture. He regaled me with how this area used to belong to his people and tales of how they hunted, farmed, and fished the land for centuries. I logged most of our discussion in my scholar's journal so that I may share the detailed information with our anthropology department upon our return to the university while retaining the privacy of this personal journal.

After the sun had set, the hunters had yet to return. Michael and I sat around the fire, drinking coffee and speaking of legends. Michael's stories were of fantastic beings residing in this forest and the Great Lakes that aided the people of the land. He also spoke of the malevolent creatures of the areas but kept from going into details or sharing the names of the creatures. However, he strongly warned that not all the creatures of this area were kind. Some were quite wicked.

"Give me the names of all these creatures, good chap." I had pressed him for more information, but he turned his attention back to the fire, ignoring the question. He would not speak of them. Then I asked if the bad creatures were what had him walking so closely beside us, fully armed.

His reply: "You should fear those creatures more than the animals of the woods. Out of all the beings and spirits of the forest, the one who craves human flesh, who exists in a constant hunger with an appetite that is never sated, is the one to be feared the most."

Michael's stories ceased when the hunters returned carrying only firewood. They had found no food. Anger was etched across their faces, yet they said nothing.

I now lay in my tent, trying to convince myself to be brave. Tomorrow, I shall insist we return to Grand Portage. While the biology department chair will not be pleased to hear the expedition has been cut short, I will let him know that in the days we journeyed, we did not find evidence of mountain lions in this forest. It is safe to assume the population to be extinct from this area.

November 29, 1923

The irony was not lost on me that today was Thanksgiving and we were nearly out of food. I approached Warren about our situation. He went on the attack, and we argued for a bit before he attempted to have the final say by stating that we would finish this trip, even if it meant losing a man or two along the way. Michael, Pinkerton, Matthews, and Georges sat in silence when I pulled my authority by saying the expedition was over and we would head home in the morning.

An air of venomous anger seeped from Warren. He said the only way he would take us back was if I promised to pay him and his men in full for the two weeks, because the decision remained mine to cut the trip short. I told him I had no authority to make that promise but would seek that level of compensation from the board. My word was not good enough, and he stormed off with his gun, taking Pinkerton and Matthews with him. He left Michael behind. Before departing, Warren had words with Michael. I do not know what was said, but Michael sat by the fire, ignoring us for the day. I told Georges I bet my bottom dollar that Warren told Michael not to commiserate with us any further. Georges agreed. He then told me that during the argument with Warren, a look of relief had crossed the others' faces when I demanded we head home. I knew we had those men on our side. I needed to think of a way for us to abandon this endeavor using their support. I refused to hike any further unless it was in the direction of Grand Portage.

We spent the remainder of the day and evening silently around the fire, drinking coffee but eating nothing. A small amount of hardtack remained, which we tried to conserve for our next hike, hopefully in the direction of the town. The johnnycakes went moldy and were discarded for the birds.

The hunters returned later that night, predictably empty-handed. No one said a word. Clouds rolled in at around nine, covering the light of the moon and casting us into darkness. The wind picked up; the temperature dropped. Please, God, do not let it snow. The fire must remain our source of light and heat for the night.

———

November 30, 1923

A heavy snowfall struck in the middle of the night. We had to dig out our tents and a small area to relight the fire. The fire aided in melting the heavy snow in the camp. Michael had the foresight to put firewood in his tent to keep it dry. Georges and I wanted to start trekking home this morning after the snowstorm ceased, but Warren warned that more snow approached; he could feel it in the air. He convinced us to stay another night. We would never make it if we tried to hike out today.

As we reestablished the camp by clearing the snow, I found the little food we had left was missing. Someone had taken the remaining hardtack. We blamed each other, and no one admitted to what he had done. I knew it was Warren. His eyes were darker, with a wild look that glinted in the firelight. He would be the one in the group I distrust the most.

I don't have the heart or the energy to write anymore tonight.

———

December 1, 1923

Warren is missing. He was not in the camp when we all woke. Pinkerton said he probably went hunting, but Matthews said Warren left his gun in his tent. Michael said nothing as we discussed Warren's disappearance and just stared into the fire solemnly and unmoving. He sat that way until Georges mentioned making coffee. That stirred him to break his eyes away from the blaze and set about scooping clean snow into the coffeepot.

After downing their cups, Pinkerton and Matthews grabbed their guns and said they were off to look for Warren. Michael muttered something about Warren being no longer with us. The two hunters glared at him and left camp without a word. Georges retired to his tent, complaining of a headache.

As Michael and I sat huddled under blankets by the fire all day, I tried to see if he knew anything about Warren's disappearance. He replied that I should be wary of Warren should we meet him and again repeated that he was no longer with us. With that, he said nothing more to me and continued staring at the fire, ignoring my questions and conversation. His cryptic message had me contemplating the meaning well into the night. This current situation has heightened my fear about our current predicament.

The wind had picked up shortly before dinnertime, just as Pinkerton and Matthews returned empty-handed and without Warren. We only had coffee for dinner. As we were finishing up, snow had started to fall lightly, and we all turned in early to escape whatever onslaught of weather was brewing.

Whether or not Warren has returned, we shall leave this damned forest tomorrow, with or without all the men in tow.

—

December 2, 1923

If anyone finds this journal, know we have perished from hypothermia or starvation. I do not know how much longer we will survive. I am cold and hungry. The snow fell heavily during the night, and we spent the day digging out camp. It is too deep for us to walk today. Pinkerton, Matthews, Georges, Michael, and I sit around the fire, bundled in blankets and nearly leaning into the flames to capture its warmth. Warren did not return, and we will not look for him. It will be too risky for any man to step away from the warmth of camp.

———

December 3, 1923

Michael is gone. His pack and gun are gone. The only evidence that he was even with our party is his tent, which still stands, and it holds the remaining firewood. A godsend, for sure—had it been left out, the wood would have been soaked from the snow. Pinkerton and Matthews do not react to his disappearance, saying that Michael always does this and will be back, but something in my gut does not think that is true. I believe this group of men will never see Michael ever again. No one could make it that far back to town without food.

Georges woke late. He came out of the tent complaining about his stomach and nausea. With what little coffee we had left, we made a pot and passed around a cup to share, each man getting about two sips before the cup was empty.

The four of us emptied the contents of our packs, and the only food we could come up with were three stale cookies that Georges's wife had given him before we left. Luckily he had forgotten about them due to his initial excitement about this adventure or he would have eaten them by now. We quartered one and saved the other two for later.

The hunters left camp not long after that to search for food. With the snow thick and nearly knee-deep, Pinkerton and Matthews nearly crawled on all fours as they left camp—a fruitless act on their part. No animals will be out there if they can barely walk in the snow.

After continued complaints of not feeling well, Georges returned to his tent to lie down. I took it upon myself to clear the camp of the accumulated snow, banking it up behind the tents as a windshield, but left a path open that the hunters tended to take between Michael and Pinkerton's tent.

———

I was not surprised that Matthews and Pinkerton returned at dusk empty-handed. Shivering and blue-lipped, they huddled around the fire. The wood stores dwindled, so after I cleared the snow from camp that morning, I searched for whatever wood I could find that didn't require me to swing an ax too much. With depleted energy, felling a full tree was not an option. Michael's tent is full of broken branches and small limbs that I could easily split.

None of us acknowledged the low grumbles emanating from each of our midsections. Hunger constantly hovered over our heads.

Georges did not come out of his tent tonight; however, I did peek in before retiring, and his soft snores let me know that he was fast asleep.

———

December 4, 1923
To wake with a cold, burning pit of hunger in my stomach while in a tent surrounded by snow is the most uncomfortable situation I have ever been in. The constant gnawing tugs at my attention, and I struggle to distract myself. Even while writing this journal entry, a hollow fire burns, calling out to be fed. I'm scared. I don't know how much longer I can hang on.

We will become ghosts, haunting the trees and the land. I can almost see us weaving around the tall tree trunks as gossamer wisps of our past selves. As I watch our future play out in my mind, my shadow against the tent wall, illuminated by my dying candle, beckons me with a wave, calling me outside. I'm not ready to give in. Not yet.

Thank God there hasn't been any more snowfall since the last storm.

—

December 5, 1923

Warren returned tonight, his eyes wild; his skin had gone a sickly gray. He walked about the camp muttering indistinguishable words and his body manic with twitches. We were all unsettled by the man's sudden return and crazed nature. God only knew where he had been and what had happened to him. The men murmured about him being bewitched by supernatural beings that haunted the woods. I think the man has gone mad and found a fallen tree to sleep under until the snow died away. Supernatural beings . . . a bunch of nonsense.

Matthews coaxed Warren to sit by the fire and prepared to wrap a blanket around his friend's shoulders. Before we could react, Warren's arm lashed out and slashed Matthews's throat. We saw no knife in his hands and had no idea how he made such a brutal cut through flesh without a weapon.

Pinkerton clocked Warren hard on the back of his head with the butt of his rifle, rendering the man unconscious. A deep gash spurted blood from Matthews's neck, but we were able to wrap it up with his scarf to stop the bleeding. Pinkerton then tied Warren up in his tent. I walked Matthews to his own and laid him down. Georges, hearing the commotion, crawled out of his tent and, despite still looking sickly, offered to sit by Matthews all night to keep watch that the wound did not bleed out.

I do not have much hope for Matthews. Maybe it would be a godsend to let Warren kill him. He would be out of his misery and free from suffering the same fate that haunted this camp with the threat of death by starvation or hypothermia.

———

December 6, 1923

Snarls and hisses seep through the fabric of Warren's tent as he remains bound inside. I can't bring myself to look in his direction. Instead, I stare past the minuscule fire I'm attempting to keep alive with twigs and small branches—the remains of our wood stores. We will run out of wood tomorrow. I know my future self is still out there, haunting the trees. I can't see him, but his voice is loud and clear, whispering in my ears: "I'm hungry; oh, so hungry."

I tried to ball up my hands to rub my eyes, and while my right hand did well to comply, the digits on my left hand have become ghastly white and nearly immobile. The pain of my hand distracts me from the ever-growing hunger in my stomach. My gloves disappeared yesterday after Warren returned. I want to say he stole them, but I'm in no mood to go into his tent to seek proof.

———

Pinkerton has stopped speaking. When he comes out to the meager fire, he's silent and stares at the small flames licking at our last bit of wood. I assume Georges is still in Matthews's tent. I do not know if the injured man is alive or dead. And I cannot muster up the energy to walk across the camp to look. There is only enough left to take me back to my tent.

14

December 7, 1923

My ghost haunts me. He stands on the edge of camp, just beyond the perimeter, and whispers suggestions on survival. Somehow, I have kept my right hand from getting frostbite but neglected my left hand. My fingers are black. Dead.

"It's meat," my ghost whispers. Everyone is in their tents as I burn the final bit of wood. Soon, all our heat will be gone. There is no more wood to obtain. It's all wet. All wet.

"Sate your hunger," my ghost says. In that moment, I held my left hand to my face and contemplated if my blackened fingers would be satisfying.

December 8, 1923

Someone stole the fingers on my left hand. Blood splatters on the tent floor. Someone stole my fingers.

Monsters are growling outside my tent.

Be careful.

December 9, 1923

All dead; we are all dead. The snow, tainted red with blood. I have resigned myself to lie among the corpses.

—

January 30, 1924

I have not been able to bring myself to write since that cold, gruesome day in December. As the sole survivor, I must detail an account of the last day of the Grand Portage excursion to honor the dead.

—

None of us had the strength to walk in the deep snow. We never left camp. During that final night, I believed myself to be dead. Despite being bound with every ounce of clothing I had brought along, I woke the coldest I had ever felt in my life. Somehow, I stood and stumbled out of my tent; soft moans and gurgles beckoned me.

Red painted the pristine white snow in our camp. It was vibrant. Pieces of the bodies lay scattered about the common area. Matthews and Pinkerton—entirely dismembered. I could not figure out which arm or leg belonged to whom. In a delirious state, I staggered into the midst of the mess. At that moment I took notice of a man crouched in the center of the massacre. He had his back to me but wore Warren's shabby buffalo hide jacket. The seams of this coat were split at the shoulders and back as if this bulkier man had struggled his way into the garment.

His body oddly twitched as his arms moved in front of him. I could not see what he was doing with his back to me. Along with the jerky movement came a wet snapping and tearing sound. As I walked around, I gave the man a wide berth, slowly drawing out a long hunting knife from its sheath at my right hip—a gift my father gave me on my twelfth birthday. But I digress.

Unfortunately, as I had not watched my foot placement, I lost the element of surprise. A large crunch caused me to break focus on the man and look to the ground. I found myself standing . . . oh, God, how I dread to write these words. . . . I stood inside the torn-open chest of Georges. He was hollow—his organs gone. My foot snapped his damaged ribs like twigs.

The man snarled, and I looked up at him in terror. His eyes were Warren's, but the rest of his face had transformed into something inhuman. A dark gray snout jutted out, lined with mangled sharp teeth. He stood to his full height—several feet taller than Warren's actual stature. From his long, skinny claws, a leg dangled.

What happened next is something I am still in absolute disbelief over. "What have you done?" I yelled at the creature who used to be Warren. The tone surprised me, being more of scolding than of shock or horror. Yet that tone may have been what saved me. Something softened in Warren's eyes, and he looked at the scene about him, dropping the leg he chewed upon. With a mournful howl, he ran off into the forest and left me standing amid the decimated bodies of my team.

Once I controlled my shock, I took whatever supplies I determined to be of use and could carry, which was difficult now, being fingerless on my left hand. Michael's gun and Pinkerton's heavy clothing were the first things I collected. From Georges's pack, I took his compass. I wanted to find his wedding band to return to his wife, but I could not bring myself to dig through the carnage. Before I departed, I pushed the tents over to cover most of the murder site—the best burial I could give these men.

I knew Grand Portage stood south and trekked in that direction. I did not make it far before exhaustion fetched me. I fainted not too far from camp. To my vast luck, not too many hours after I collapsed, Michael showed up with a small search team and came across my body as they headed toward the camp. They were sure I was dead, my body stiff and nearly frozen, yet they found a pulse when they checked. Michael saved me. The group carried my frostbitten body for two days to Grand Portage and delivered me to the holiday home of a Minneapolis-based surgeon, who took me in and tended my wounds.

None of my saviors saw hide nor hair of Warren. They did find the massacre, but because of the desecration of the bodies, the search party was not prepared to carry the remains out of the forest. Furthermore, due to the onslaught of snow this winter, the authorities have indicated they would not attempt to collect the dead—or whatever remained—until spring, after the snow thawed. They said it was not worth risking people's lives to retrieve corpses. I knew the remains would never be found, and those men shall never be given a proper burial. From what I learned of Warren within those few days stranded in the forest, his greediness would entice him to return to our desecrated campsite and finish his meal.

———

I have made a full physical recovery despite missing a few toes to frostbite and the fingers on my left hand, to what I can only surmise to be a hunger-induced delusion. However, after the horrors I witnessed deep in the forest of Grand Portage, I do not believe that, mentally, I will ever be the same again.

Gray Magic

"My mom's gone and left me with my stepdad. He doesn't treat me very well. For Christmas I had asked for a PiePaddy 7 tablet for school since, with everyone being sick, we had to be at home. But he bought me school clothes instead! Why would he buy me clothes if I still have to stay at home because of COVID?" Sebastian Johnathan Blatt sniffed, and a tear slid down his cheek. Molly's heart ached for him. "How long has your mom been gone, Sebastian?"

"Johnny, everyone calls me Johnny."

"I'm sorry. Johnny. How long has your mother been gone?"

"About three months."

"Are you here because you want to talk to her?"

The corner of Johnny's mouth twitched, and he said nothing more. Molly assumed he was holding back his emotions about his mother. That he couldn't come to bring himself to say that she had died. Molly reached out and clasped his hand. She knew how Johnny felt. In her heart, she knew that he wanted to speak to his mother one last time. She didn't have to ask him.

19

"No young child should ever experience the loss of a parent." *Nor should a parent experience the loss of a child,* she thought as she reflected on her own life.

"My real dad died in a car accident before I was born. My stepdad's the only father I've ever had."

"I'm so sorry, sweetheart. Do you want to talk to your father too?"

"No."

Floored at the fact that Johnny had lost both of his parents, Molly didn't press the issue or inquire how his mother had died. She sat back in her rocking chair and looked up at the painting of Caireen, which had once hung in her daughter's bedroom and now sat above her fireplace. *This poor child. Goddess, protect him.*

"How old are you, honey?"

"Ten." He didn't look at her when he answered. Instead, he looked around her parlor. It had to have been an odd sight for him, her parlor. Hand-drawn protection runes decorated all the walls of her home, and paintings hung in tribute to the Celtic pantheon. On her coffee table she kept her crystals all displayed and rotated according to the moon's cycle. However, she was sure little Johnny was most taken aback by the sheer volume of plants that decorated her parlor. This little room had the best light in the whole house, and she used it to house her extensive indoor plant collection. Ranging from the common to the exotic, the plants were like her children, and she prided herself on how well she maintained them.

"And does your stepdad know you're here?"

"No." He now made eye contact with her. She inwardly sighed as she saw how sad and hollow his face appeared.

"Okay. I'm sorry, honey, but my fee is five thousand dollars plus a sacrifice." Johnny winced. Magic wasn't easy. Or cheap. However, she had a feeling that his stepfather could afford the price. They lived in a very affluent part of the city. "You need to sacrifice something meaningful to you in connection to your desire. But please, no people or animals."

"Five thousand dollars?" He broke eye contact with her and stared at her large *Monstera deliciosa* 'Albo Variegata'. Her pride and joy. A gift from her daughter.

Her heart sunk further. What was she doing? This child was crushed, and here she was, extorting him with the ability to speak with his deceased mother. She bit her fingernail. Her greed had gotten the better of her.

"Sorry for bothering you." Johnny stood and made his way toward the front door.

"Wait!"

Johnny turned. Tears dripped from his face.

"Don't worry about the payment—my gift to you. Just bring something to sacrifice. But before you leave, I need a lock of your hair and a few fingernail clippings."

Johnny stepped back, holding onto his hands; a disgusted look crossed his face.

"It's okay, sweetie. I need a part of you to initiate the ritual. Nothing bad will happen to you by my using these items."

"Okay, ma'am." Johnny let go of his hands and allowed Molly to lead him to the hallway bathroom. She removed a pair of shears and nail clippers from the medicine cabinet. Pulling a tissue from a box on top of the tank of her toilet, she laid it down on the sink and then picked up the clippers. Gently taking Johnny's hand, she clipped some of his nails off his right hand and placed the clippings on the tissue. She repeated the action with the shears and his hair, taking the smallest lock the ritual would allow. Once complete, she folded the hair and nail clippings in the tissue and placed them in the front pocket of her apron.

"There you go, all done. Now that was painless, right?"

"Yes, ma'am," he said, shuffling behind her as he followed her from the bathroom to the front door.

"Come back in three days. I need to prepare for the ritual. Can you be here at two in the afternoon?"

Johnny smiled for the first time since he had walked through the front door of her little brownstone.

———

Three days later, at 2:00 p.m. on the dot, there was a knock at her door. Johnny stood there, soaking wet from the pouring rain. Molly ushered him in and helped him remove his rain jacket and galoshes.

"Good thing you are only a few blocks away." She tapped him on the nose and smiled. He'd found Molly online through her latest social media advert about her craft of giving people what they desired—within reason. While she had the power to conduct a ceremony that granted any desire, three requests would cause her to turn away the requester, as they went strongly against her morals: murder, forcing unrequited love or non-consensual sex, or for the dead to be brought back to life. However, speaking to the dead was entirely within her remit, and she was happy to oblige this young fellow.

Molly had practiced solitary witchcraft and served her community, the prestigious Rittenhouse Square, with spells-for-sale for over forty years. Most knew what she did, and they left her in peace to do as she pleased because they either needed or feared her. Only the rich could afford her services, and she preferred to cater to that level of clientele. Their desires were more pragmatic, practical, and not all about money. Mainly because they could already afford to buy their material needs. The needs the rich brought to her were on an emotional, mental, or spiritual level. Some wanted security. Others wanted peace. Most wanted increased levels of success or fame.

The rite to grant these wishes was easy, and sacrifice was key. It must be an item of the most personal, heartfelt connection to the desire—an eye-for-an-eye situation.

However, asking Molly to perform the ritual was not without risk. Requests must be exceptionally specific, or one wouldn't get what they wanted. But it is up to her client to be precise. Molly cannot provide guidance. As part of her pact with the being who granted the desire, she would never give her client guidance or interrupt a ceremony. And by agreeing to this, Molly was given the power to deny the three types of requests that went against her morals.

Not being able to provide guidance was hard to keep quiet about. Last year, a man wanted his mother's Alzheimer's to "go away." And that's exactly how he asked for it. A moment after the man stated his desire, he received a phone call that his mother had died. The woman's death technically wasn't murder. Molly, who foresaw this outcome based on her initial screening of the man, had stared at the floor during the entire summoning, fighting the urge to correct his statement.

Molly's rituals bordered between white and dark magic. She dubbed it "gray magic." Her craft required her to call upon a being not of this dimension. And she had been known to dabble in necromancy. Several years ago she bound herself to an entity from Purgatory because that realm too dabbled in "gray." It was neither Heaven nor Hell and, therefore, was not swayed by good or evil.

Molly's binding with her entity was not something typically done. Usually, others like her would summon various entities from other dimensions versus binding themselves to a specific one. Molly wasn't keen on that because she didn't want random entities doing her bidding. She tried to get to know her entity and maybe establish a partnership with them. However, most don't bind an entity to themselves because the act carries significant risks, such as becoming manipulated by the entity over time. Molly believed that is how most possessions occur, though those who are possessed refuse to admit that they were dabbling in binding summoning spells in the first place. So she was always keenly aware of what she was doing and performed only the safest ritual with her bound entity, Anamanbháis.

23

In all the years she had dealt with her entity, she had never been able to determine if the being was a demon, an angel, a god, or something else. She'd done many thorough searches online or through old books but never found any information on the being. Sometimes Molly wondered if she had created it herself. But that was a silly notion, as she assumed that Anamanbháis was quite powerful.

Molly led Johnny to her dining room and then went into the kitchen.

"Would you like a cup of tea?" she asked through the doorway.

He smiled and nodded. "Two scoops of sugar, please."

A tremor in her chest caused Molly to take a sharp breath. That was the same way her Ami drank her tea.

As the water boiled and she readied a pink cafe cup with a tiny gray kitten on the side with a tea strainer full of calming lemon verbena from her garden, she heard the boy start to hum. It was a soft song. One that Molly remembered she used to sing to her daughter when she couldn't sleep: "Somewhere over the Rainbow." Molly's hands shook as she poured the boiling water over the tea strainer. She hissed as a little splash of hot water hit her hand. A welcomed—despite painful—distraction from the memories of her daughter as a child. She ran a finger over the cup's handle, happy that a child was once more drinking from the kitten cup.

Molly finished the cup of tea with the requested two scoops of sugar and pulled a shortbread Scottie cookie from a tin out of her cupboard. She took the steaming cup into the dining room and placed it along with the cookie in front of the boy. He looked up to her, smiling.

"There you go. Drink this and warm up while I prepare the rites. Come to the room at the back of the hallway when you're done, and then we'll begin.

Johnny smiled at her before grabbing the little shortbread cookie and dunking it in the tea. Molly chuckled and walked out of the dining room toward a first-floor bedroom she had converted to conduct rituals. She didn't want any of the magic of the ceremony to infiltrate the rest of her house. Sometimes, "stuff" was left behind after the summoning that took days to clear with sage and prayer. Stuff being left behind usually occurred when the requester asked for something selfish or sinister. Molly tended to be quite good at vetting potential clients, typically meeting them three days before the summoning. However, there had been instances where a requester asked for something completely different from what was discussed during the vetting process. While a rare occurrence, it did happen more than Molly liked. She hated being lied to. Her defense was limiting the magic to this room, since she couldn't interrupt the rites once it started. The runes written on all the walls in her house kept the magic here, contained.

Molly took a piece of white chalk off her altar and drew sigils on her waxed oak floor, finishing off by drawing a large circle to contain the sigils. While admiring how neatly her lines were drawn, she felt herself being watched and looked up to find Johnny standing in the doorway.

"Ready?" she asked. He nodded.

She picked up a heavy and worn tome. Leather bound—or at least she hoped that to be the material. A spell book passed down through her mother's lineage.

Johnny scuffed his toe on the floor as he looked down.

"Can you hand me what you want to sacrifice?"

He looked at her. Tears welled in his eyes. "The most important thing to me was the last thing my mother got me. My birthday is January 1st, and she bought me my PiePaddy 7 when my stepdad wouldn't get me one for Christmas."

Molly's chest tightened. She wanted to scoop him up, hold him, and make his pain disappear.

"Ma'am, I can't part with it." And with that, Johnny fell to the ground and sobbed.

Oh, how her heart broke. She needed to do something for him. This child needed to speak to his mother one last time. To say his goodbyes. Molly put her spell book down and knelt next to Johnny. Pulling a handkerchief from her pocket, she handed it to him.

"Dry your tears. I think I have a solution. Wait here."

Molly went up to her third-floor bedroom. She retrieved a gold ring engraved with Celtic knots from a jewelry box. It was the last gift she had bought Ami before she passed away from leukemia at thirteen. The ring was warm to the touch. Molly could never bring herself to call on Anamanbháis to grant her deepest desire—to speak to her daughter one last time. Ami would disapprove of her mother's use of magic for her own gain. But she may be able to sacrifice this token in order to have Johnny speak his desire. After all, the ring would be a sacrificial representation of a bond between a mother and child. She would use his fingernails and hair to bind him to the ritual. *This should work.*

She returned downstairs, but before going back to the room, she entered her parlor and picked up her *Monstera deliciosa* 'Albo Variegata'. The last plant her daughter had bought her. The one that Ami had spent all her birthday and holiday savings on as a cutting of this specific variation can cost upwards of two hundred dollars. While it pained Molly to depart with the plant, it might benefit Johnny by enhancing the sacrifice.

When she entered the ritual room, plant and ring in hand, Johnny sat cross-legged on the floor outside the summoning area. For a young boy of ten, he was well-mannered and quite polite. His mother had done an excellent job of raising him.

"Let's start. Just stay seated where you are. Once the rite is complete, a being will join us in the center of the room within those sigils. Don't be afraid of it. It's nice. Once it asks you what you want, precisely say your desire. You must state very specifically what you want, okay? That is all the guidance I can give you."

"Why?"

Molly giggled at the boy's question. Typical child, always wanting to know reasons. Ami's favorite word as a child had also been "why." This sweet boy's demeanor reminded her so much of Ami.

"Because to have the ritual work properly, only the requester can ask for their desire. Your desire wouldn't come true if I interfered by giving guidance or help to clarify your want. That is because it would no longer be your request alone, and this gift I am bequeathing to sacrifice on your behalf would be lost in vain."

Johnny nodded his head, and with that, Molly opened her spell book to a well-worn page and began the ceremony with an incantation.

She then placed her daughter's ring on a large stone offering plate and the *Monstera* beside it. The gold ring melted into the stone as she spoke, and the plant flashed in a blaze. All that remained of the *Monstera* was a pot full of dirt and ash. Molly sprinkled the dirt, ash, and Johnny's fingernail clippings and hair on the melted gold. Anamanbháis's sigil appeared inscribed on the stone's surface above the sacrifices. It had worked. Sacrifice accepted.

Once she completed the incantation, the lights in the room blipped. She and Johnny were cast briefly into darkness. A smell of brimstone filled the air. When the lights came back on, Anamanbháis sat hunched on thin legs with arms wrapped around knobby knees. The dark gray fur on its body hadn't been cleaned in a while, becoming quite matted. Molly "tsked" at the unkempt look. Anamanbháis looked at Johnny with its white pupilless eyes.

"This the kid?" Anamanbháis's voice was two-toned—masculine, deep, and husky with higher feminine notes. As it nodded its head toward Johnny, the two furless, fleshy appendages that started at the top of its head and traveled down the back to fall over its shoulders and hang over its arms (much like a young girl's pigtails) swayed with the movement. Johnny stared wide-eyed back at the being. Molly prayed that Johnny wasn't terrified. She wanted to reach over and give him a reassuring pat on the shoulder, letting him know everything was okay. But she couldn't interfere.

"Yes," she answered.

"Whaddya' want, kid?" It spoke more informally to Johnny than usual, making Molly happy. It was trying to show Johnny it wasn't so scary.

Johnny stood, never taking his eyes off the entity before him. As he reached his full height, Johnny folded his arms across his chest and leaned back against the wall.

"Listen here," Johnny started. "I know how this works, so I'm going to be specific about what I want."

Initially startled by how forthright Johnny spoke to Anamanbháis, Molly couldn't help but smile at the child's boldness and preparedness. Sacrificing her most sacred totems of Ami had not been wasted.

"I want two million US dollars to appear in a Nassau bank under Brendan Finn Hackton's account. That's my stepfather." Johnny placed a piece of paper on the floor and slid it toward Anamanbháis. The paper moved past the sigils and into Anamanbháis's hand. "The routing and account numbers for the bank account."

"Very well—"

"Hold up." Johnny put a finger in the air as he stepped forward toward Anamanbháis. "I'm not done."

"You desire more?"

"It wasn't specified that there was a limit for how many things I could ask for. She said I could ask for whatever I desired."

Anamanbháis laughed. "Go on."

Molly stared at the child, her mouth hanging wide open.

Johnny pulled a folded sheet of lined notebook paper with torn edges from his back pocket. He unfolded the paper and said, "I want my stepdad's company headquarters moved to Deimos, Pennsylvania, where my mom has her mountain house in the Poconos, and I'll live full-time in that house from now on. I want the house renovated to look like this." Johnny set a picture cut from a Colorado ski magazine outside the circle. With a flick of a wrist, the photo shot through the air and was caught in Anamanbháis's hand.

"Lovely," it murmured. The house sat alongside a lake surrounded by tall, fluffy conifer trees. The house itself had seven gables and a turret.

"A witch's tower," Johnny said as he explained the specifics in the picture, right down to the three river stone–encrusted chimneys, Craftsman arched beams, and hand-hewn logs that held the structure erect. "And I have my own floor in the house that is nothing but a game room. There is to be a fifteen-foot-deep pool in the backyard that has a diving board, a slide, and a waterfall grotto. Also, throughout the forest, behind the house, are mountain bike trails that are all mine. No one else will ever use them. I want a Yeti SB150 T3 Turo mountain bike with DT Swiss EXC 1501 Carbon wheelset and SRAM XX1 Eagle AXS. I want the latest Xbox gaming system that perfectly runs every Xbox game that has been made and will ever be made. When I'm eighteen, I want a free education at Massachusetts Institute of Technology. After graduation, I want to be the greatest geneticist to have ever existed, making my stepdad proud of me. And finally," Johnny looked right at Molly. "I don't want that old witch there to remember any of this because I don't want to owe her five thousand dollars. Plus, she's fully responsible for any negative consequences that my request may cause now or in the future. It's her sacrifice, after all."

Anamanbháis erupted with laughter and raised its hands, about to clap. "So mote—"

"Wait!" Molly stepped up next to Johnny. "What about your mother?"

Anamanbháis held up a finger. "I'll let this interruption slide."

"Oh!" said Johnny. "Yes. I want a Tiffany and Company legacy bracelet for my mother. Packaged in the iconic Tiffany's box wrapped with a Tiffany blue silk bow. It is nearly Mother's Day, after all."

"Wait, wait, wait," Molly said. "You said your mother's dead."

"No," replied Johnny. "I said she was gone. I never said she was dead. She got arrested for selling her company's trade secrets to their top competitor." He turned to Anamanbháis. "Though she needs to stay in jail. I kinda got the run of the house whenever my stepdad travels for his job."

Molly's hands shook as the blood drained from her face.

"I like this kid." Anamanbháis clapped its hands, granting all of Johnny's desires.

"No! He's just a child. He doesn't understand the consequences," Molly gasped.

"You mean *your* consequences?" Johnny gave her a smile and scuffed over the chalk line with his foot as he walked to the door—breaking the circle she'd drawn to contain Anamanbháis. "Bye, Molly!"

"Stop! You have no idea what you've done." And honestly, she had no idea what Johnny had done in releasing Anamanbháis because she knew next to nothing about the being. But deep down, she knew that nothing good would come of this.

"Ta-ta," Anamanbháis said, raising a scraggly, black-clawed hand in a half wave as it levitated off the floor and followed Johnny out the door.

"Wait," Molly hollered, hurrying after them. The moment she stepped outside the door, her vision distorted and a wave of nausea washed over her. She leaned against the doorjamb, rubbing her eyes with closed fists to clear the stars. When she dropped her hands and opened her eyes, she stared down the empty hallway toward her front door.

Confusion rattled her—she couldn't remember why she had just been in her ceremony room. The lights were on when she looked back into the room, and a partially erased containment circle marred the floor. *Funny*, she didn't remember having a client today. And she certainly didn't remember drawing that containment circle.

Maybe she had forgotten to clean the floor after the client she had last week. Molly tsked herself, annoyed at her forgetful memory. "Molly, old gal, it's time to start drinking your ginkgo tea again."

Of Sharks and Dreams

Seated on the weathered dock bench, the little blond-haired kid was a dead ringer for Alfie Merek's son, Parker. Alfie pulled the hood of his sweatshirt lower over his eyes, not wanting to risk being seen as he looked at the boy. Alfie had loved it when Parker was that young; six-year-olds were full of innocence and wonder. At thirteen, Parker had seemed interested in Alife's life as a lobster fisherman. Ecstatic at the prospect of his son being his first mate, Alfie took him out of school—against Parker's, his mother's, and the school's wishes—and they were on the boat every morning at 4:00 a.m. But his kid grew up too quickly, and as Parker reached sixteen, he had become bored of this little Maine island.

It was everything Alfie could hope for, having his son by his side. However, this little harbor town and Alfie's dreams couldn't contain Parker. His son wanted so much more out of his life, with aspirations of being a marine biologist and studying chondrichthyans.

"Stop using those scientific terms and just call them sharks. There is no need to give those beasts silly Latin names that no one remembers or can say. They're just sharks." Alfie had often said something of this nature to Parker when he started to go all "scientific." It was annoying and caused the kid to lose focus on the job at hand—setting or pulling in lobster traps.

"Chondrichthyes is so much more than just sharks, Dad. It's a complete classification of animals, including rays and skates. And . . . ," Parker started a scientific argument to refute his father's claim. "There is so much unknown about the creatures. They have many unique evolutionary advancements that we've barely scratched the surface of understanding them. Advancements that'll help us grow technology and health care. Plus, they are as old as the dino—"

"Enough! Your head is full of nothing but sharks and a dream you'll never achieve. Focus on what means something to the world. What we do—we're feeding people. Giving them sustenance to keep them alive."

Parker would then add some planet-loving comment like "I hardly see how overfishing our oceans is good for our planet" to provoke Alfie.

But Alfie never took the bait, because when he did, Parker would mope at the bow of the boat for the rest of the morning, ignoring Alfie and his responsibilities.

No, college would be a waste of the boy. Marine biology isn't a career. Parker believed he'd become some grand scientist, but in reality he'd just be chumming the waters while some other egghead did all the scientific stuff and made the big bucks.

Parker would learn what he needed to understand about the ocean by being a lobsterman, with Alfie as his teacher. There was no need to spend tens of thousands of dollars at a college when good old seafaring hard work and labor—actual hands-on experience on the open waters—was the best way to learn. Alfie had forbidden Parker from rejoining high school when his son protested about not being enrolled, saying that Alfie was preventing him from achieving his dreams.

Parker had disappeared when he turned seventeen after a fit of rage.

Alfie never knew where his son had gone until about a year after Parker's disappearance, when he received the phone call he'd prayed he'd never receive.

When Alfie and his wife, Beth, identified Parker's body, the track marks were visible in the crook of his right elbow. His body had been found with a needle still in his arm, almost six hundred miles away on a dirty mattress in an alleyway between the old Five & Dime store and a greasy pizza shop in some random northeastern Pennsylvania mountain town.

Beth left Alfie shortly after, placing all the blame for Parker's death on him, for she swore that Alfie only ever loved the sea.

That was never true. Alfie loved the sea *and* his son. He wished he could turn back time and tell Parker that he loved him, wanting his innocent six-year-old Parker back. He would do anything to hold his son again. Anything.

"I can take you to see a real baby shark," Alfie lied as he stood next to the child whose head was bent low over a PiePaddy tablet that played a video about a yellow baby shark and his family. He assumed the kid's mother was the woman who stood at a nearby Saturday morning farmer's market stand on the pier, purchasing the fresh catch of the day from the new fishmonger in town.

Alfie eyed her warily before returning his focus to the kid. The kid beamed up at Alfie, excitement swimming in his big green eyes. Then he nodded his head and stood, reaching for Alfie's hand.

Alfie felt disconnected from his body, like he floated outside of it and observed himself taking the child's hand and walking to the *Salty Lady*. He took a quick look around. No one had seen him; better yet, no one had recognized him. The weathered boards of the bobbing dock beneath his feet groaned with the shift of the wind. The sea beckoned him. Alfie knew he shouldn't have come back to Stonington. But something called out to him to return. Called him home.

Questions were asked across Alfie's community—questions about him. He'd run away after body parts of two young boys washed ashore last year on different occasions—one child in spring and the other in summer. The rumor mill said he was the last to be seen near the boys when each was alive.

The questions weren't wrong. Alfie had invited those boys on his boat. They also reminded him of Parker. But those kids had been mistakes. They turned out not to be Parker.

Once Alfie realized that he had made not one but two wrong selections, he had left Maine for some time. He became transient up and down the Northeast coast, catching and selling what he could to make enough money for food and diesel, lying low and out of sight of the law.

Alfie suffered nightmares about his son's demise, but when the horror of his son's death one day turned into peaceful dreams, Alfie believed that his son had returned and was waiting for him in Stonington. In his bones, Alfie felt and believed that Parker's soul had found his way back home.

The kid walked hand in hand with Alfie toward his boat, chattering about sea life as the "Baby Shark" tune continued to play from the device clutched in his tiny hand. Alfie was confident that this time he was right. This kid's fascination with sharks was the same as Parker's.

He is Parker. I know it, Alfie thought, and he smiled as he lifted the boy off the pier, placed him in the faded, paint-peeling *Salty Lady,* and then hopped in after him. There was no doubt in his mind.

Alfie took the boy to the cabin and sat him on the floor beside the steering wheel. "Stay here until I get the boat cast off and we are at sea. The waters are choppy, and I don't want you to fall overboard." He lied. The little boy smiled at Alfie and nodded before returning his attention to his PiePaddy. He'd keep the boy out of sight until they sailed beyond Stonington's harbor.

As Alfie uncoiled the anchoring ropes from the dock, screams came from the direction of the fishmonger's stand.

"Maria. Maria! What's wrong?" Alfie heard the fishmonger shout. His gnarled, sea-weathered hands quickly worked harder to uncoil

35

the aft-port rope from the pier before tossing it in a pile onto the *Salty Lady*'s floorboards. He'd recoil it later.

"Ricki! Ricki!" Alfie saw the woman running down the docks, screaming for a boy, looking at every boat, coming closer to Alfie's.

"Mommy?" The sweet, soft voice came from the cabin. Alfie turned and saw Parker standing in the doorway. Alfie leaned a leg over the gunwale of the port side and pushed away from the dock, then hurried to the cabin as he saw the woman starting to run in his direction. She screamed for him to stop. Alfie blocked the kid from seeing his mother by lightly grabbing him by the shoulders, spinning him back into the cabin, and closing the door behind him.

"Is that my mommy?" the kid asked.

"No, Parker. Your mommy left." Alfie grumbled as he turned the key, and the diesel engine roared to life. Images of Beth flitted through his mind.

"My name isn't Parker," the kid sniffed. "It's Ricki, and I want my mommy."

Alfie angled the *Salty Lady* away from the dock and into the harbor. Sliding the port side window open, he stuck his head out. The woman stood at the pier's edge, screaming toward Alfie's departing boat. While he couldn't hear her over the roar of the *Salty Lady*'s engine, he was sure she was calling out to her son. He shivered at the thought of the woman screaming for "Ricki." He imagined that her cries were hauntingly similar to Beth's as she had cried Parker's name when they identified his body. Cries of a distraught mother who realized her child was gone.

He needed to get out of there fast before Harbor Patrol appeared. A bead of sweat dripped from his well-worn ball cap, stinging his right eye. He could do this. He could get away with this. Alfie would make it seem like he was heading south, but as soon as he was out of sight of land, he'd head east, toward Nova Scotia.

There was a tug at his overall pant leg. Alfie looked down to see Parker looking up at him, fear etched across his face.

"What's wrong, kiddo?"

"My mommy was calling me."

Alfie's hands shook on the wheel as a lie spilled from his lips. "Yeah. She was, but I talked to her. She told you to have fun seeing the sharks with me."

"But she didn't say bye to me," Parker sniffed.

"She did from the dock. You must not have heard her. Are you ready to see some sharks?"

Parker bit his lip, and Alfie saw the kid was mulling over whether to be happy or throw a fit. He was still maneuvering out of the harbor and couldn't tend to the kid.

"I want to see them," Parker said as he hit "Play" on his PiePaddy and started playing the video he was watching.

"Good, now go sit over there on that stack of blankets in the corner. We're heading out to sea!" Parker complied.

Good kid, Alfie thought, rationalizing that he had made the right choice. Those other boys he had thought might be Parker had fought him the whole time as he took them to sea. They bit and screamed and threw things at him. They called him names and told him his boat was stupid.

Alfie was embarrassed that he had thought one of the other kids could have been his son. He was annoyed that he'd made the same mistake more than once. The best thing Alfie could do for himself and the ones he had taken was to abide by his promise to show them sharks. And both times, with each boy, he lured the predators close to the boat with chum. While the boys were mesmerized by the feeding frenzy, he'd picked them up and put them in the water to swim with the sharks, giving them the same dream Parker had always wanted.

Aside from the chugging of the diesel engine and the music coming from the kid's device, silence filled the cabin. He stole a quick look at the kid. A smile was etched on his face.

"Very good," Alfie whispered and continued course, soon finding himself safely out of view of the land. Better yet, there were no Harbor

Patrol or Coast Guard boats in sight. Alfie turned his boat sharply to the east. His brother lived in Newellton—a half-day trip—and with the *Salty Lady*'s diesel tank filled that morning, they could make it. He knew how to get around Border Patrol. Alfie had traveled to Toddy's place often and had yet to check in with Canadian Customs and Immigration. Getting around the government was easy, though he and Parker would have to lie low at Toddy's for a bit.

His brother now had his nephew back. Toddy would help him and the kid. Hell, Toddy would let them live there because his brother knew the pain Alfie had suffered when Parker died.

"Whatcha watchin', kiddo?" Alfie asked once they were well on their way to Newellton.

"Baby Shark," the kid said, but the shark sounded more like "shirk."

Alfie chuckled. "Turn up the volume so I can hear it, and lemme see."

The kid stood up, walked next to Alfie at the wheel, and held up his PiePaddy so they could both see. The kid turned up the volume and restarted the song. Alfie cringed as two dancing kids sang an irritating earworm of a tune as a colorful family of sharks danced across the screen.

"You know, 'em sharks been around since the dinosaurs." Alfie thought it might be good to tell the kid something interesting about sharks that his son once told him.

"I know that," the kid said without looking away from his tablet.

"Oh." Alfie shifted uncomfortably on his feet, not sure what else to say.

The video ended.

"Again?" The kid smiled up at him, little green eyes sparkling. Parker's eyes were brown, but this kid still looked nearly identical.

"Sure," Alfie answered, smiling. He'd do anything to appease Parker.

———

The sun was high, and it was a little after noon. The kid had to be hungry. Alfie brought him some peanut butter crackers he found in his lunch box. He'd never been one to stock the boat properly with food. When the teenaged Parker had worked on the boat, he often complained about not having anything to eat, expecting his father to supply the food. That always miffed Alfie. It wasn't his job to be sure Parker was fed. He was only to provide the money. Beth's role was to feed him despite her dictating that parental roles would be shared fifty-fifty. However, Alfie recalled that she only said that when it suited her. In other instances, she demanded complete control. Like when it came time to name their son, she insisted that the baby be named for a long-dead relative from Minnesota who went on several expeditions across the United States in the early 1900s. Despite the many stories about uncanny events he had experienced, Beth stated that it would be lucky to name their son Parker so that he might have a lot of adventure in life. Attempts to remind her that the guy had died while locked away in the Duluth asylum had fallen on deaf ears.

"I have to do it differently this time," Alfie muttered to himself as he gripped the worn handles of the ship's wheel. He'd have to take care of Parker alone—well, with Toddy's help after they arrived in Newellton. Alfie had to make it work this time—for him and for Parker. He wasn't going to lose his happiness this time.

But that song. That damned "Baby Shark" song just kept playing over and over again. He gripped the wheel tightly as the kid sat on the floor next to him, replaying the song for the five millionth time.

Then there was silence. Alfie turned his head to see the kid slapping the screen with his hand, tears welling in his eyes.

39

"Where are you taking me? I want my mommy!"

The moment the PiePaddy and "Baby Shark" died, the trance that he and the boy were in shattered. A void opened in Alfie's stomach. The kid realized he'd been taken.

"Take me home to my mommy." The kid waved his dead PiePaddy as a tantrum ensued. This was the part of childhood Alfie hated; little kids could be so irrational.

"Listen to me, Parker."

"Noooooo," the kid howled. "That's not my name!"

Snot dribbled over the kid's lip and he licked it away. Alfie gagged and then fished a handkerchief from his pocket. The kid fought him as Alfie tried to wipe his face.

"Mommy!" the kid stomped his feet. "Take me to Mommy!"

"Looky here, kiddo. I brought you out here to see Baby Shark, remember?"

"Baby Shark is here?" He sniffed. "But my mommy."

"Knows you are here with me and wants you to have fun. And Baby Shark is out there, though we stay quiet and watch for him." Alfie motioned for the kid to follow him to where his lobster traps were stacked. "Stay here. I'll be right back."

The kid seemed to have accepted Alfie's lie and looked over the boat's gunwale, dropping his PiePaddy to the deck boards. It bounced away from where he stood, and Alfie shook his head at how indestructible the devices were nowadays, coming in their own waterproof, shockproof, sealed case.

"Don't lean over the edge too far or you'll fall overboard, and Baby Shark will eat you."

The kid jumped back and crouched to the floor laughing, singing the lyrics to the song about being safe.

Alfie chuckled at the creative use of the lyrics. Parker was always such a brilliant kid.

A bucket of his secret-recipe lobster chum, made of bits of fish and shellfish soaked in chicken blood for two days, was in the small fridge in the cabin, and he retrieved it. The smell always punched him in the face when he retrieved the old metal bucket from the fridge he kept running on a portable generator. He prepared himself for the rank odor of rancid and rotting crabs stinging his nostrils as he opened the door.

When Alfie returned to the kid, he sat on a lobster trap, hunched over and hitting his PiePaddy screen.

"Dead," he said and held the tablet up to Alfie.

"It's okay. You're about to see something really cool!" He took the dead tablet out of the kid's hands, set it down on top of the stack of traps, and then held up the chum bucket. The kid made a face as though he was about to be sick.

"Throw up overboard," Alfie snapped, but the kid swallowed hard. Color bled back into his face. With a dipper, Alfie scooped some of the chum and threw it in the water. The gore hit the surface of the water and quickly floated behind them.

"Christ! We're still moving." Alfie, dropping the bucket on its bottom—sloshing some of the chum out onto the floorboards—and ran back to the cabin to stop the boat. The enjoyment of being with Parker had intoxicated him, and he was utterly ignorant of what was happening around him.

As Alfie ran to the cabin, he looked back at Parker and saw him pick up the bucket, turn his head away from the stench, and stand beside the gunwale. The bucket was too heavy to hoist up over the railing, so Parker climbed the stack of lobster traps. Torn between pulling Parker off the traps or stopping the boat, Alfie ran backward, keeping his eye on the kid—the boat needed to be stopped. As Parker climbed with the bucket and Alfie sidestepped into the cabin's doorway, the boat's hull slammed into something hard, stopping it before Alfie could stop the *Salty Lady* himself.

Alfie's forehead cracked against the doorjamb, knocking him down onto the deck. As his vision sparkled with a thousand stars and before everything went black, he saw the top lobster traps pitch toward going overboard, with Parker and the chum bucket standing on top.

———

Thrashing and dull thuds against metal woke Alfie. Gripping the door-jamb, he pulled himself up. The world tilted about him, and he worried that his vision was going. Pain throbbed at the back of his head, and he touched where it hurt. Feeling the wetness in his hair, he pulled his hand away to find the fingers and palm covered in blood. The boat listed toward starboard. His vision wasn't messed up. He'd hit something.

Parker!

Alfie ran aft to where the lobster traps stood. They toppled all over the deck, with two falling overboard. He didn't see Parker or the bucket anywhere. The thrashing in the water continued over the side of the boat.

The void in Alfie's stomach spread into his chest as he went to the gunwale and looked over the side. Blood tainted the water, and Alfie felt his heart rate spike. The chum bucket floated amid the feeding frenzy, bouncing around with the thrashing shark bodies. There was no sign of Parker. Relief washed over Alfie until something reflective, black, and rectangular floated in the water, catching his eye. While the sharks had missed it, he didn't miss seeing the PiePaddy.

He leaned forward over the gunwale. The kid would have never let anything happen to that tablet. He had to have gone in after it. Parker . . . he had lost his son all over again. Alfie screamed up at the sky.

"Parker. PARKER!" Hot tears streamed from the corner of his eyes and down his cheeks. The void had now grown into his throat. Alfie had never felt so empty before. The PiePaddy continued to float amid the frenzy, catching the sunlight and reflecting it onto Alfie's face. He needed it. Alfie needed the PiePaddy. It was the last thing of Parker's.

He reached over the edge of the *Salty Lady*, fingers outstretched toward the device. A massive thud portside where the sharks were feasting shifted the boat, dipping Alfie toward the churning water. Alfie grasped onto the railing and hauled himself back up. And that is when he noticed that he had rammed into a red metal buoy.

Leaning back over the railing on the side that was sinking, he could see a hole where the buoy had punctured the hull. The boat was taking on water.

The PiePaddy bobbed in the red waves amid shark tails and fins. Alfie scanned the deck around him and saw nothing he could use to grab the tablet. He again leaned over the gunwale, reaching for the device.

"Parker. Parker, please!" Alfie sobbed. A shark's nose-bumped the device, moving it further from Alfie's reach.

"PARKER!" he yelled. A small wave crested and pushed the device back toward Alfie. He leaned further over, grasping the edge of the gunwale with his left hand and balancing atop the rail on his hipbones. His right leg was up in the air, his left foot barely connecting with the floor. His body rocked and bobbed in motion with the sinking boat. The tip of his finger touched the PiePaddy.

"Oh, Parker, please," he cried.

"I'm not Parker!" the shrill scream came from behind him right before he felt his left ankle being grabbed and lifted. Alfie lost balance, tipping forward into the thrashing red waves. He didn't lose grip on the railing, but his bottom half was fully submerged, legs bouncing off solid bodies that whizzed through the water. Alfie looked up and saw Parker there, glaring at him.

"Parker—please! Help your daddy!"

"You're not my daddy! I'm not Parker!" Parker's face was beet red, with tears streaming down his cheeks. He bit Alfie's right-hand fingers that clung to the top rail of the gunwale. Alfie kicked his feet and howled at the pain as he dropped his arm, fingertips grazing the water's surface to wash away the pain. Just as he reached back up to the railing to pull himself up, blinding sharp pain enveloped his wrist, followed by a sharp tug and a release. He lifted his arm to find blood gushing from the stump at the end. His entire left hand was gone.

Alfie looked back up at Parker, who glared at him. While fear seemed to be in Parker's eyes, Alfie couldn't help believing that a smile tugged at the corner of the kid's mouth.

The crimson waters, further darkened by Alfie's blood, exploded around him. With his tiny fists, Parker started pounding at the fingers on Alfie's left hand. Alfie tried to maintain his grip and, with his feet, walked up the side of the boat to climb back aboard, but the blows from Parker loosened his grip on the *Salty Lady*'s railing. As his body crashed through the crimson surface of the Atlantic Ocean, razor-sharp teeth found purchase in his right thigh and dragged him down to the depths of the sea.

Little Maise

"But why can't I do things like this?" Maise asked her parents, who looked at her with strange looks on their faces.

"Because it's wrong." Her mommy knelt beside her and turned Maise's head away from the animal. Behind Maise, a kitten lay gutted and decapitated. Her father handed Mommy a handkerchief. Maise noticed the look of anger in his eyes. Once white, the cloth soon turned red as Mommy wiped the blood off Maise's hands and face. Maise looked at the small lines creasing Mommy's face as she smiled.

"She needs to be taken care of." Her father stared at her as he spoke.

"Oh, she'll be okay. Won't you, baby?"

Maise nodded as Mommy wiped the last streak of blood off her face.

"There, all clean," Mommy said as she lightly tapped the tip of her finger on Maise's nose. Maise giggled but stopped when she looked at her father's eyes.

"She isn't normal."

"She'll be okay," Mommy replied.

———

A man came to her in her dreams again that night. He held Maise tight with warm arms and whispered comforting words of love and protection.

My little angel. My little Maise, he said to her before she woke. For the past year, he has visited her in her sleep, trying to convince her that her parents weren't her own. That he was her real father and that he'd take care of her. Not like the man who lived in her house who claimed to be her father. That man was a fake.

But her mommy. She loved her mommy.

Why don't you and your mommy come live with me? I'll take care of you both forever. We will be a family.

Maise wanted to go with this man and bring Mommy with her. To get away from who she thought was her father as he treated her and Mommy badly. He yelled a lot. And sometimes Mommy would have bruises.

The man asked Maise to do little tasks for him so that he could come to get Maise and her mommy. He'd asked her to send him a kitten.

So that you have a pet when you come to live with me.

———

Maise woke to the smell of pancakes and bacon—her favorite.

Mommy smiled as Maise walked into the kitchen, rubbing the sleep from her eyes. Her father sat at the table, hidden behind a newspaper. He didn't look at Maise.

Mommy talked with her throughout breakfast about going to the park later in the day.

46

"I think it is time we take her back to the lab." The newspaper didn't move as her father spoke.

"Going out would do her good."

"She shouldn't be out in public. Tests need to be run."

Her mommy stopped drinking her coffee and held the cup to her lips; her eyes looked sad. "Sebastian . . ."

Her father put the paper down and leaned in toward Mommy. "She needs to be returned to the lab so I can make sure what's going on here isn't happening to the other kids."

"But it doesn't matter if it is happening to the other kids. They are not ours. She's ours."

"What other kids?" Maise whispered. Mommy put the mug down and smiled at Maise before opening her mouth. But no words came out.

"No, she's property of Thenurgee," her father said.

Her mommy stood and cleared the table. "Maise, go upstairs and get dressed to go to the park."

Maise smiled and started to go upstairs. As soon as she was out of sight from the kitchen, she sat on the stairs to listen to her parents talk.

"I created her. I can damn well do what I want with her." Her father's voice sounded angry.

"She's *ours*."

"No, she isn't. She's the product of my DNA and sacrifices." He coughed. "Next week she's returning to Thenurgee's genetic lab for tests. Based on the results, she'll be fixed or destroyed."

A sob from Mommy made tears build up in Maise's eyes. She never liked Mommy being sad.

"Come off it, Claire. She's just a body. Bodies can always be created. I'll make you a new one."

"You can't just 'make a new one.' I want Maise. She's mine."

"No, she isn't. Not one ounce of your DNA is in her. She's property of my company."

Mommy started to cry. Maise wanted to comfort her but didn't dare to have her father catch her listening.

"Stop crying. The whole reason I created this company was for you. To get you a kid."

"Don't say that."

"It's your fault that we can't have kids."

"That's not fair. How can you say something so awful?" Her mommy's voice cracked.

"We started something here, and it is a lucrative business. I'm not going to let one defective child ruin it. You can have one more week with her, and then she goes back. If she's salvageable, I'll return her."

"She's not a car off the assembly line or a defective toaster, Sebastian; she has a soul!" Mommy sounded angry.

"Get real. You're honestly going to start spouting that shit about souls being the magic to life? You know full well that it's the body naturally waking after gestation and the brain directing the body to do what it's programed to do. No divine spirit imbued itself in her, jumpstarting her life. For Maise and the other kid, we were the jumpstart. We made the spark that brought a wad of DNA and flesh to life."

"Not me. You and . . . and that devil did." A clatter of dishes made Maise jump.

"We don't speak about Anamanbháis!" her father shouted, "Besides, if souls were real what kind of soul does an eight-year-old who kills cats have?"

"It was an accident, Sebastian, and this discussion is over. She stays here with us." At the sound of footsteps heading toward her, Maise silently climbed the stairs to her room and softly shut the door. Tears streamed down her face as she trembled, understanding Mommy and her father's fight.

The man who had been visiting her in her dreams was right. Those two downstairs weren't her parents. So that must mean that the man in her dreams is really her daddy.

———

Maise sat on the swing, watching her mommy sit on the bench beside Mrs. Bealy. Mrs. Bealy had just had Gene, but the more Maise thought about it, she never saw Mrs. Bealy have a big belly. Maybe Gene was one of those other kids her mommy mentioned. A kid like her.

Her mommy took Gene from Mrs. Bealy's arms and held him close. Maise felt a twinge in her heart because she wanted to be held right now by her. She wanted Mommy to tell her that what she overheard wasn't real. That Maise *was* her daughter.

But what you heard is real. A slight breeze tickled Maise's ear. She turned to find out who spoke to her, but no one was behind her.

You can't see me right now, but I am here.

"Who are you?"

My little Maise, it's me—your daddy.

"Where are you?" Maise's heart pounded in her chest. "Are you a ghost?"

He laughed. *No. I'm somewhere you can't understand, but I can come to get you if you'd like.*

"How do I know you are my real daddy?"

Because I'd never treat you like the man who lives at your house.

"He ignores me a lot. He doesn't love me like Mommy. She's my mommy, even if I didn't come out of her belly, and she tells me I'm her 'everything.'"

You are right. She truly loves you. But he doesn't love you, and he never will.

Maise believed the man because, in her dreams, this man treated her better than the man who lived in her house did.

49

"Do you know my mommy?" Maise pointed to where Mommy sat. As Mommy looked at Maise, a weird look crossed her face. Maise watched her give Gene back to Mrs. Bealy and then walk toward the swing Maise sat on.

I'll be meeting her soon, but don't tell her about me. I need you to do me a favor. I will tell you tonight when you dream.

"Why can't you tell me now?

No answer.

"Hey!" She turned and looked behind her again.

"Maise?" She turned around on the swing to find Mommy standing right in front of her. "Who are you talking to?"

Remembering what her daddy said about not telling Mommy about him yet, she said, "No one."

———

Maise was playing with her trucks in the living room when the man in the house walked in. He went past her, sat on the couch, picked up the remote, and turned on the TV.

"Do you want to play with me?" she asked him. He didn't even look in her direction.

"Excuse me?" She tapped his leg to get his attention. The sting across her face registered in her brain before she realized he had slapped her. Tears filled her eyes, distorting her vision as she looked at the man. A sharp metallic taste flowed onto her tongue, and she swallowed.

"Go to your room, and never hit me again."

"I didn't hit you; I was trying to get your attention."

"Go to your room!"

Maise ran from the living room, passing Mommy, who had hurried over to her at the sound of the yelling. Maise pushed past as she ran up the steps and to her bedroom.

"What did you do?" Maise heard her scream. The man screamed back at Mommy, but Maise blocked what he said as she slammed her bedroom door shut and crawled under her bed.

———

Maise wanted to fall asleep so she couldn't hear the yelling and screaming from downstairs. Mommy and the man were fighting. She couldn't hear what they said but knew it was about her. Eventually, the arguing stopped and she heard crying. Maise wanted to go downstairs to hug her mommy but was afraid to leave her room.

The sounds of footsteps coming up the stairs made Maise slide back further under her bed, closer to the wall.

"Maise?" There was a soft tap at her bedroom door before it opened. Her mommy's feet appeared, and then she knelt to find Maise in her hiding spot.

"Come out, honey."

Maise shook her head.

"Baby, please come out." A mug appeared on the floor, and then her mother reached for her under the bed and held onto her hand. Warmth flowed through Maise's body as she allowed herself to be taken from her hiding spot. Her mother gathered her in her arms and rocked Maise, humming a lullaby she used to sing when Maise was younger. It had been a few years since she'd heard the song. She didn't resist when a mug of hot chocolate was placed in her hands. She listened to her mother's melody as she drank the yummy chocolate. With each mouthful, she swayed her head in tandem with the song, and soon her eyes became heavy.

———

The coldness of her bedroom shocked Maise awake and she shivered. The stark white of the walls made her afraid because her bedroom walls were a soft blue. She sat up, and the thin white sheet that covered her slid down, revealing a nightgown that wasn't hers. The room was empty save for the mattress she lay on. *The door . . .* Maise felt a lump form in her throat. She recognized the door: all gray metal with a small window—a small window that people would look through at her. She remembered being stuck in this room before but couldn't remember when.

The springs of the mattress creaked as she crawled off it, and the moment her feet touched the floor, she recoiled from the coldness. This room wasn't safe. She couldn't remember why, but she'd been here before and was very unhappy. Gathering her courage, she put her feet firmly on the floor, allowing the cold to shock her again. When she became used to the cold, she quietly tiptoed over to the door. Grasping the handle, she found that it wouldn't move. She was locked in. The metal was chilly against her hands as she slapped her palms against the door.

"Let me out! Let me out!!" No sounds came from the other side of the door in answer to her pleas. She continued to yell until her voice cracked.

Feeling like she couldn't scream anymore, she whimpered, turned her back to the door, and slid down to sit on the cold floor. With her knees to her chest, she wrapped her arms around them, buried her head, and sobbed.

My little Maise.

Maise snapped her head up and turned to the door. "Are you there?"

I'm here, my child.

"Oh, please. Let me out of here. I want to go home."

I'm sorry, but I cannot do that for you.

"Why?"

Don't ask questions you don't want to hear the answers to.

"I don't understand. I want to go home."

Sweet child, you are home . . . technically.

"No, I'm not! This isn't my bedroom. These aren't my clothes. Take me home!"

Just be patient, little one.

"Where is my mommy."

Would you like me to sing for you?

"No! Help me!"

There was no further response.

"Hello?"

No one spoke to her from the other side of the door.

She stood, ran to the door, and slapped her palms against it over and over.

"Hello? HELLO?" she screamed. The metallic thuds of her pounding filled her ears, and soon a headache began to hurt behind her eyes. With a sob, Maise turned her back to the door and slid down to sit once more on the icy floor.

Alone, she wept and breathed in. The room smelled of nothing. Her home usually smelled of pumpkins or apples because Mommy liked to burn those kinds of candles. Those smells made Maise feel warm. This smell of nothingness made her feel cold and hollow.

Maise returned to the small mattress opposite the door, curled underneath the thin blanket, and cried herself to sleep.

———

Maise sat upright, clamping her hands over her ears; she woke to the screams of sirens. She began to shake out of coldness and fear as the blanket fell away. There was pounding coming from outside her door. A muffled voice echoing beyond the door could faintly be heard above the shrill.

"Maise!"

Her mommy!

Maise jumped out of bed and slapped her hands against the door. "Mommy! I'm here!"

There was a beep and the door swung open. Her mommy stood before her. One eye looked sad; her other eye . . . a huge bruise stood out large and purple on her cheek, and it puffed up so badly that it squished her other eye closed.

The sirens in the hallway went quiet. Outside the door and down the hallway, Maise heard the man who lives in her house calling out to Mommy.

"Oh, baby. I'm sorry. Come on." Her mommy knelt and reached out to Maise, and Maise ran to her. Her mommy wrapped her arms around her body and pressed her face to the top of Maise's head.

"I'm sorry, I'm sorry, I'm sorry," her mommy said.

The man appeared behind Mommy and she let Maise go. He glared at Maise then breathed hard, rolling his eyes. "Can we hurry up here? I want to go back to bed."

"Sebastian, she's scared."

"Yea, well, it's your fault. You're not allowed here anymore. *You* set off the alarms by breaking into my lab."

"I came to get my child."

He grabbed his hair with both his hands and growled. Then, exhaling hard, he said, "She doesn't belong to you."

Mommy turned to look at the man. "If you don't let me take my child out of here, I'll go to the press and tell them what you and your *devil* have done here."

The man punched the door, the sound echoing in the room. Then he started to laugh. He stepped toward Mommy. "Go ahead, I dare you. No one will believe you."

Maise stepped back into the room. Mommy looked scared, then swooped forward to grab Maise again. Maise felt herself melt into Mommy's arms as she was lifted from the ground. Mommy carried her out of the room, past the man, and down the hall.

"Let's go home, baby," Mommy said.

———

Are you hurt?

"He hit me yesterday before I went to sleep, but Mommy made me feel better. Though I had the strangest dream of being somewhere else. And Mommy saved me."

Mommies are lovely creatures. However, be careful when dreams aren't dreams.

What he said sounded weird. Mommies weren't creatures, and Maise was pretty sure the room she was locked in was only a dream, but she nodded in agreement. Though the dream felt very real: The cold room. The sirens. Mommy and the man. The car ride home. The yelling from the man outside of the car when Mommy drove her away from him. The sniffles coming from the front seat.

But she woke up in her bed, in her room, and in her PJs that morning. So it had to be a dream. Though Mommy's eye was bruised and puffy this morning at breakfast . . . just like in her dream.

Would you like to come with me?

"Yes, but what about Mommy? I need her to go wherever I go."

I told you that she can come with you.

"Really? When can we leave?"

You can leave tonight, but you must do something first to reach where I am.

"What do I have to do?"

Remember the kitten?

"Yes. You asked me to send you the kitten."

Correct. You must do the same with your mommy. Send her to me, and that will open the door to my house. Then you and your mommy can come live with me.

"Do I have to do the same thing to Mommy as the kitten?" Maise felt uncomfortable. She didn't want to cause her mommy any pain. The kitten was easy because she didn't know the kitten, and she did as her daddy instructed by breaking its neck first before cutting it open to spill its blood onto the ground. The kitten felt no pain.

Are you afraid?

"I don't want to hurt Mommy."

I promise she won't feel any pain. You'll be setting her free. That man in your house will only get meaner and start hitting you both more.

"I won't let him!" Maise grew angry at the thought of the man hurting her mommy. "What do I have to do?"

There is a bottle of pills in that man's cabinet that says "Oxycodone." Put two pills in your mommy's nighttime drink. Once she falls asleep, do to her what you did to the kitten.

"Then me and Mommy can come live with you?"

Of course, my little angel. Now listen closely to what else you must do to open the door after you send me your mommy.

———

Maise listened to her mommy stumble up the stairs and head to her bedroom after drinking her nightly drink. She heard the man downstairs yelling at her, calling her a "damn drunk."

Maise slipped into her mommy's bedroom and hid in the closet before Mommy got into bed. Earlier that day, she had hidden the big butcher knife from the kitchen in the closet. No one knew it was missing. She took the knife from its hiding place and tiptoed up to her mommy's side of the bed. Only the light on Mommy's nightstand was on.

"Mommy?" Maise lightly shook her. She was sound asleep. Maise crawled up on the bed and straddled her mommy, who lay on her back. Maise pulled up Mommy's shirt to expose her soft stomach. Maise pinched Mommy's skin to be sure she didn't feel it. She didn't wake up.

Raising the knife high above her head, she shoved it down hard into Mommy's stomach. Just like with the kitten, Maise pulled the knife downward, cutting open her Mommy's skin. Blood gushed from the wound. Mommy moaned softly but never moved. Maise pulled open the incision and began pulling out her Mommy's insides because it would make more blood. Her daddy said there needed to be a lot of blood for the door to open.

Maise crawled off Mommy and went to the closed bedroom door. She drew a symbol on the back of the door just as her daddy told her to do. Once done, she whispered, "Anamanbháis, toghairm mé thú."

Mommy coughed as her breaths became slower. Maise stepped back from the door but continued to watch it, waiting. The moment Mommy stopped breathing, the bedroom door opened; Maise squinted, for the light from the hallway was exceptionally bright.

A figure soon blocked the light and stepped forward. All the lights in the bedroom flickered on, and before Maise stood her daddy—tall and dark and covered in dirty-looking fur. Two white eyes, like big white dishes, stared at her. The stench of rotten eggs filled the room. With two humanlike arms that ended in claws, he reached for Maise.

"My little angel. My little Maise."

Maise dropped the knife, ran over to Mommy, grabbed her limp hand, and then turned to look back at the doorway.

"Little one, you just have to do one last thing before we can leave," her daddy said.

A smile stretched across Maise's face, and she nodded her head.

"Pick up the knife. The man downstairs. Do the same thing to him, and this door will fully open for you and your mommy to come with me."

"Okay, Daddy!" Maise exclaimed.

Identity

My friends haphazardly threw together this idea of a hiking trip during the lowest point in my life. Thank God for Ellie and Sheena. They saved me from a very dark place. A place where I didn't know who I was, and didn't believe I would ever find myself again. Sheena decided that backpacking for two days would distract me from my misery. Ellie agreed. Both arrived at my dreary apartment one Saturday afternoon to pull me out of bed and drag me down to the basement, where my camping gear collected dust in a storage unit.

Seeing my outdoor equipment strewn about the floor did not quell my misery. The gear was all newly purchased within the last year. My lying, thieving, now ex-boyfriend had sniffed at my father's camping supplies, which I'd inherited after Dad passed away when I was eleven. I had let the ex nudge me into spending thousands on what he called the most cutting-edge gear, after which he left me alone to decide what to do with my father's hand-me-downs. Eventually I stashed the old stuff in a couple of totes in the back corner of my storage unit, behind my bikes and seasonal clothes. There it remained. While my father's legacy lay relegated to its

59

plastic basement-corner grave, an oblivious Sheena and Ellie went gaga over the new gear.

"Amelia!" Ellie shrieked, pulling the tent from its unopened box. "This is perfect! Just big enough for the three of us." I gave her a half smile. Kurt had fought with me about that tent. He wanted a two-person ultra-lightweight model priced a couple hundred more. My claustrophobia won that battle—it helped that I was paying—and I had purchased the less-expensive, four-person tent. It's a bit too heavy for backpacking, but Ellie suggested we take turns carrying it.

"You have everything here," said Sheena. "Tent, cooking stuff." Her voice went up an octave as she clutched another box. "Oooh, an outdoor shower!" It wasn't anything glamorous. Just a vinyl hide with a water bladder, and the water would be cold as hell. Heat rose in my face and traveled to my chest, where I was starting to feel something. I had managed to keep all this stuff after the event with Kurt. We never did go camping, but now I was going to be able to use it all for the very first time with my best friends—my saviors. For the first time in months, I was feeling better. A little more than a notch up from awful, but it was something.

———

At 8:00 a.m. we left our little town of Deimos; my bank sent me its daily text message of insufficient funds. Huddled in the back seat of Sheena's little blue Honda, I turned off my phone. My stomach soured. Kurt was locked up in jail, eating three meals daily, while I couldn't even afford an apple. All my money was tied up in litigation after he'd robbed me blind, stealing my savings and identity. It had been five months, and I still had not recovered.

"You okay?" Sheena asked. She watched me from the front seat, eyes squinting into the rearview mirror. Her copper bangs covered the outer corners of her blue eyes, making them pop, and hid her laugh lines. I couldn't tell if she squinted from a smile or concern.

"Yeah." I turned to the window, jealous of her hair—vibrant compared to my dull blonde color. I was not happy that she had decided to drive. Sheena and Ellie were paying for everything. Aside from the equipment, they wouldn't let me contribute. Not that I could have afforded the trip. These days, everyone was picking up my tab. Without a glance back, Ellie sensed my darkening mood; my burgeoning happiness from yesterday was gone—done in by the text message from my bank. I heard the smile in Ellie's voice. "Amelia, you need to lock all your pain in a box right now and put it away for the weekend. You're with us; we'll take care of you."

Tears stung my eyes; she constantly told me how to control my emotions. How could I be happy? Mom was covering my rent, paying out of Dad's life insurance, though she only did so because my sister, Mia, harassed her. Since Dad died, Mom had mentally abandoned Mia and me, hiding away in her bedroom and never lifting a finger to care for us—her children. Until this shit show happened in my life, I had cared for Mia. Now the tables have turned. My sister gives me money for food and supports me during my breakdowns, which is sickening to think about, as I'm the older sister. Yet I need her. . . . Whatever I make from work goes right to bills and an attorney.

"Those fucking legal fees," I mumbled.

"Amelia—" Ellie started.

"Just stop. I have nothing and am nothing right now. Thanks for what you are doing for me this weekend, but I can't just turn my happiness on like a switch."

Ellie turned in her seat and looked at me, her dark brown eyes comforting, but I was still unsettled. "I know how you feel."

"Ellie," Sheena hissed.

But it was too late. My voice leveled, and somewhere inside I died. "How can you know how it possibly feels to have the first man you have ever trusted steal all your money and everything that identifies you as you? My Social Security and passport numbers are splattered across the dark web for eternity, and I have to fight for a new identity. I am damaged for life." Silence hung in the space between us, drowned out only by the roar of the road underneath. "I have to prove that I'm the victim!"

My voice lost its energy. Ellie sulked in the front seat, but I didn't care. "You have no idea what it is like to lose yourself and then have to fight to create a new identity."

———

We arrived at the trailhead somewhere in the Appalachian Mountains of Pennsylvania. I had not paid much attention to where we were going. As Sheena and Ellie argued over the trip's details the day before, I sat on my couch and stared at the camping gear scattered about the floor. I vaguely recalled the plan to hike fifteen miles, camp overnight, and hike fifteen miles back—a two-day trek. That would be enough for me. I did not want to be away from the comforting confines of my apartment any longer than that. Sheena had the most backpacking experience, and I was okay with her telling me where to be and when.

On the other hand, Ellie seemed to fight Sheena in every way, asking, "How will we know we are in a safe place to camp?" and "Where will we get water if we run out?" and various other questions that annoyed Sheena.

Sheena had showed up bright-eyed at 4:00 a.m., Ellie in tow in the passenger seat. Sheena had said reaching the trailhead would take a couple of hours. The summer temperature would not go above 75 degrees Fahrenheit. But no one had thought to check the weather forecast for rain. When we arrived, the parking lot was mud. So much for Sheena-the-outdoor-woman. While clearly it had rained all night, now it was blue skies overhead, and Sheena figured we were clear sailing from here on out. Shivering, I pulled the hood of my jacket over my head, thanking God this thing was water-repellent. That had been Kurt's idea too, though I stopped short of giving him credit.

"Okay, ladies," Sheena said with too much excitement. "I've downloaded our route, and we're ready to go." A blue device glowed in her hand.

"Do you have a map too?" Ellie nodded her head toward the device. "That thing needs batteries."

"It's rechargeable. And I have a fully charged power brick. Plus, we all have our phones. It's 2019, Ellie. No one carries paper maps anymore."

She lied. On those survival reality shows, people usually had maps on them. Yet I don't care, as the trail should be clear enough to follow. Her GPS was for show.

We slopped our way to a faded sign with an arrow pointing into the woods. The morning light barely filtered through the trees. Taking one last look at Sheena's car, I stepped into the dark forest after the two of them.

———

The terrain was rocky and grueling. Occasionally, one of us would stumble over a rock or tree root. Heavy breathing wheezed from our lungs, and I could see a rivulet of sweat running down the back of Sheena's neck after she tucked her long hair into her cap. Trees seemed to lean in on us as we trekked, trying to choke us out. "It's spooky here," Ellie said. Sheena spun around and held her hands high, fingers splayed like claws.

"I vant to suck yer blood, blah." Ellie shrieked and ran around Sheena, who in turn chased her. A chill went up my spine.

"Be quiet," I hissed, but they didn't hear me and continued acting like loud morons. I hunched over, pulling my arms tight across my chest, scanning the forest.

"HEY!" Sheena jumped in my face. I screamed and stumbled back. "What's your malfunction?" she asked. "We are just having fun."

I straightened up and looked at her. "I feel like there's something out there."

"That's just your paranoia," she said, slapping my shoulder and stepping back. "Sorry, Amelia, that isn't what I meant. Look, there's nothing here. No one's spying on us, not even the animals. There hasn't even been a bird."

Ellie appeared next to Sheena. "She's right. I haven't seen a bird or even a squirrel," she said, trying to distract me from the fact that Sheena had called me paranoid. "Isn't that weird? No animals."

"Eh, it rained this morning, and everything's a mucky mess," Sheena said. "The critters all stayed home." Ellie laughed. I pouted, soured by the paranoid comment. We continued walking the trail. Ellie and Sheena carried on, obnoxious, their voices filling the void of silence that cloaked the forest. I followed behind, my hands clenching my pack's shoulder straps. I could not shake the feeling that we were being watched.

———

The hike up the mountain was an endless train of switchbacks. But as we ascended, the feeling of being watched subsided. When we reached the top, we came upon a surreal view. I looked out across the expanse, awash in a sea of greenery. Solid trees and hills rolled ahead as far as the eye could see. Since we'd started the hike, the sky above had gone from blue to a dull, hazy gray. Saturated rain clouds hung thick over the mountain peaks about ten miles away, obstructing our view of anything beyond.

"Those rain clouds look to be moving east," Ellie said.

"Yeah, we should be fine," Sheena said. I nodded but was not reassured by their assessment.

Ellie pointed toward a boulder farther down the trail. "We can climb up and see over the other side of the mountain." She ran to the boulder and scrambled to the top before Sheena and I could protest.

Sheena looked at me and shrugged. "When in Rome."

"Come on, 'Melia," Sheena called out and beckoned with a wave. I huffed and walked around the base of the boulder to the other side. I had seen too many reality Emergency Room shows with episodes about hikers climbing up precarious rocks that unexpectedly shifted under their feet. I wouldn't follow them and appreciated the few moments of silence their climb afforded me. Out in front of the boulder they stood on was a large slab of rock with smaller rocks scattered about.

Movement off to my left caught my eye; something slipped over the edge of the slab. I took a step back, unsure. It had to be an animal. I hopped across to the slab, taking wide steps over cracks in the rock, to walk near the edge. Nothing surrounded me but the sky, and I felt light as air. The thoughts of those Emergency Room shows evaporated from my mind as I took in the grandeur and beauty of the mountains.

Something flashed off to my right. I turned, hoping to catch sight of it. Another flash off to my left. Whatever it was moved quickly—a pale blur. It kept popping up and disappearing amid the cracks in the slab. I took off after it. It had to be a squirrel. That's the only animal I knew that could move so fast and squeeze itself into those tiny cracks. The little critter had me zigzagging and jumping all over. Overjoyed in trying to catch the little bugger, I found myself laughing.

"What are you doing?" The yell came from overhead. I stopped and looked up at Ellie, high up on the boulder. Sheena stood next to her, both their faces etched with terror.

"There is something down here. Trying to catch it."

"Looks to me like you are going to run straight off that rock," Sheena said. "How 'bout you come this way."

My stomach clenched—my shoe was planted just a few inches from the edge of a cliff. I took a big step backward, and only then did it sink in how close I had come to falling. Blood pulsed in my ears, drowning out all sound, and my breath stilled in my lungs. Ellie yelled at me; her mouth moved, but I couldn't hear her words.

Sheena appeared on the other side of the slab and walked toward me. Wide-eyed and frowning, her eyes locked onto mine—and I found that soothing. My lungs creaked, releasing the air I had been holding onto. I took a breath. Then another as the sweat that had broken out on my forehead evaporated. Trying to act like nothing was wrong, I laughed and said, "What—do you think I'm going to jump?"

"Come on, Amelia, let's go," Sheena said, reaching out to me as she stepped closer. Her eyes no longer looked at me but at the rock at my feet. "It's not safe."

I allowed her to grab my arm and gave up on my search for the animal. It had to be long gone by now, anyway. As I stepped toward Sheena, my foot slipped into the crack I straddled, wedging firmly.

"Only you." She leaned down and grabbed my calf. I braced my hands on her backpack to anchor. "One, two, three," Sheena counted. We pulled. A sharp crack echoed through the air, and the look that crossed Sheena's face made me think we had just broken my leg. I started to fall backward as the rock let loose from the side of the cliff.

"Shit!" Sheena grabbed the right strap of my pack and started leaning backward. The ground opened, and the rock beneath me vanished into the valley below. For a moment I dangled midair, and thoughts about starring in one of those Emergency Room shows stirred in my brain. Sheena maintained her grip, face red with strain. I tried to pull myself up, but my flailing arms made contact with nothing but air. She yanked and fell backward, pulling me across and against the rocky edge of the cliff, scraping my hands and arms. I lay beside her legs on the rock while mine hung over the cliff. Not wasting a second, Sheena changed her grip to the top loop of my pack and dragged me across the rock and back to the hard-packed dirt of the trail. She let go once I was safe and bent over, breathing hard, with her hands on her knees. I climbed to my feet, my clothing filthy from being dragged and scrapes covering exposed skin. Ellie climbed off the boulder and got to the ground when we arrived.

"Oh my God, Amelia, what were you thinking?" Ellie's anger poured out of her mouth. "Thank God Sheena was fast enough to get there. You would have fucking fallen, and fucking died!"

"I'm fine," I mumbled, inspecting the boot that had been wedged between the rocks for any signs of damage.

Sheena breathed heavily, hands still on her knees. She looked at me, her eyes burning. "Don't ever do that to us again!"

"I was just trying to see the animal that was running around—"

"There was no animal!" Sheena yelled, cutting me off. She turned her back on me and continued down the trail.

"It was an accident," I whispered to Ellie. She walked past, ignoring me.

Sheena just glared at me, her breathing slowing.

"Where's the trail?" Ellie said as she walked back to us.

"What do you mean?" asked Sheena. "We're standing on it."

"No, it's supposed to pick up on the other side of the rock slab; I don't see it."

Sheena pulled out her GPS and turned it on. The color screen flared as I looked over her shoulder. She zoomed in on our location, and the trail route appeared, skimming the cliff's edge before veering off into the forest.

"GPS says to go that way." She pointed in the direction behind Ellie.

Ellie sighed, "But where? There is nothing to follow. The only trail I see is the path we came on."

"And that's the reason we have a GPS. We'll follow the course marked on it until the trail appears again." Sheena's smug voice annoyed me, but I said nothing. There was no reason to add my two cents and irritate them even further. Ellie opened her mouth to reply then pursed her lips—a little facial gesture she made when rethinking her words.

"Lead the way, navigator," she said.

———

The descent from the summit was not as long as the hike up the mountain, leading me to believe we were on some ridge, even though we were no longer following the cliff's edge. Sheena veered off into the forest, her face never leaving the screen of the GPS. Beneath the thick canopy of trees, the underbrush was minimal, allowing us to quickly push past mountain laurel and small trees. Occasionally, one of us would get snagged by thorns. Despite hiking an unblazed path, there was no need for a machete to cut through dense overgrowth—a benefit, seeing how we didn't have one.

"It's crazy how a 140-pound girl can move a boulder that weighs tons," I joked, adding a laugh to show that my near-death experience hadn't fazed me.

Ellie stopped and glared at me. "That's not funny. A girl at my college went hiking up at a nature preserve on this trail just north of here. Halfway into it, she climbed a bunch of rocks to get a better view of the migrating hawks. The slab of rock she was standing on gave way. She was pinned beneath the rock. She died."

"Oh" was all I could say. I wanted to tell her that she had climbed that boulder without knowing if it was safe, but Ellie walked away, and I fell in line several paces behind them. One of them whispered, "This may have been a mistake." The other didn't answer.

———

After another few hours, Ellie declared that she was exhausted.

"Just another two hours," Sheena said. "We can get the last five miles in; this is the easiest part. Nice and flat."

"No, we're done. Ten miles is enough," Ellie said. She took off her pack and heaved it onto a fallen log, breathing heavily. I surveyed the wilderness around us, unsettled. The deeper we trekked into the forest, the darker it became, blotting out the beautiful mountain skyline we'd seen earlier. I didn't like it here.

"Maybe we should walk a bit more," I said to Ellie.

"No; I'm hungry and want to lie down."

Defeated, Sheena turned off the GPS, took off her backpack, and started to unload it, trying to dislodge the tent without removing all the pack's contents. When she finally succeeded, she began assembling the shelter.

"Motherfucking piece of garbage." She threw the tent poles to the ground. I went over to give her a hand. Her back was to me, and the instructions in her hands crinkled as she tightened her grip.

"Just tell me what to do," I said. Without a word, she returned to the tent poles and fitted them together. I squatted down and held onto whatever she pushed in my direction. Ellie sat in silence, watching.

———

The first raindrop fell an hour after the tent was set up and a fire started. After the first few sprinkles, the heavens opened with a torrential downpour. As soon as we got inside the tent, we stripped off our soaked clothes and piled them by the door, trying to keep the water away from everything else.

"Who wants dry pasta in some kind of spicy seasoning?" Sheena asked as she pulled a prepackaged meal from her sack. Most of what we'd packed required boiling water—impossible in the rain as we had no means to cook inside the tent. Ellie had brought fruit, and we devoured that. I had granola, but we decided to keep that until the morning—just in case. None of us had brought protein, like beef jerky.

Ellie crawled over to our pile of wet garments and untangled the mess, spreading the clothes out to dry. Sheena and I checked our cell phones—no service. I looked at Ellie's, being with a different carrier. Her phone was dead. We turned the phones off to conserve battery since they weren't usable. Sheena lay down on her sleeping bag. "Last year, I went on a cruise and a dead body was found aboard," she said. Ellie and I both looked at her. Sheena continued: "It was heartbreaking, some elderly woman. No one knew who she was or what cabin she was staying in. It was like she sneaked on board, but, honestly, that would have been next to impossible at her age."

"Um, okay," I said, unsure of where this story was headed. Nevertheless, I settled into my sleeping bag next to Sheena to listen, feeling a little better that they had decided to talk to me again. Ellie kept rearranging our wet clothes.

"Yeah, it was freaky. She had no key on her but was fully dressed in old-lady cruise attire. Some pool boy was cleaning the chairs at about ten at night and found her body. No one claimed her, and all passengers were accounted for. She was a mystery. I don't know what they did with the body." She sat up and laughed. "Wow, that wasn't the story I wanted to tell you, but it just popped into my head. I wanted to tell you about this excursion during a cruise where we went zip-lining right in the middle of a lightning storm . . ."

Sheena rambled on for several more minutes, this time about the zip-lining story, but I zoned out, thinking about that poor woman. She had died alone, like a nobody.

———

"Are you fucking kidding me?" I woke with a start. Sheena and Ellie's sleeping bags were empty. Outside the tent, Sheena grumbled something I couldn't distinguish. I crawled out of my sleeping bag and

70

unzipped the tent. Ellie stared at Sheena, who was smacking her hand against the GPS screen.

"What's wrong?" I asked as I pulled my boots on.

"Exactly what I thought would happen," Ellie said in a low voice. "This is why I asked if you had a map."

"This had a three-quarters charge yesterday." Sheena's voice cracked; she was on the edge of crying. One of her hands held the GPS unit. The other had the power brick. She violently shook both. "And this. This brick was fully charged!"

"The GPS is dead?" My head was still in a fog from being abruptly woken up.

"Duh!" Ellie's face contorted, mocking my stupid question, then reset her sights on Sheena. "This is why you don't rely solely on technology. Don't they teach you that in Hiking 101?"

Ellie's bitch side always came out during a crisis. It's her way of dealing with it.

"What are we going to do?" I asked.

Sheena sighed and pointed in the direction that we came yesterday. "Walk straight back to the cliff and follow the edge to the rocks. We'll grab the trail back to the car from there."

Ellie stormed toward the tent, roughly pushing past me as I sleepily attempted to put on my boots.

"What are you doing?" I asked as she tore open her backpack and began to haphazardly stuff the gear she'd removed the night before back inside.

"Going the fuck home."

———

A blister formed on my heel from my wet sock. It hadn't properly dried because Ellie laid her jacket on it last night. Pain lanced through my right leg with every step. Six hours straight of walking without a break had rubbed the skin raw. We never found the cliff. Without a GPS or even a compass, we were directionless. Often, Sheena and I checked our phones to see if we caught any signal, but with the phones continually searching for a connection, it wasn't long until the batteries drained empty. We were walking blind through the forest.

Silence enveloped us—a void eerily deprived of birds chirping or wind stirring the trees. It was as though the three of us were walking through another world, one where we didn't belong. The feeling of being watching started again when we left camp. Often I'd look behind us, as I brought up the group's rear. I rubbed the back of my neck when nothing aside from trees materialized.

Sheena wouldn't admit her mistake and continually reassured us that the cliff was ahead. Ellie cracked her knuckles when Sheena spoke. The anger and confusion became all-consuming, making me queasy.

I considered wandering off away from them. Not to find my way back to the car but to become even more lost. This situation didn't faze me like it should. This trip was just a distraction. As a kid, I'd fantasized about living like Sam Gribley in *My Side of the Mountain*. I wanted to escape life like Sam, because all my troubles would still exist upon our return.

———

The evening's darkness sneaked up on us, and we'd barely set up the tent before the sun fully set. Our only bit of luck was that our headlamps had charged batteries. If only the GPS used the same type of battery.

A fire was pointless, as all the kindling and wood around the camp was soaked from the rain the previous night. None of us spoke as we lay inside the tent, tucked warmly within our sleeping bags. The rain returned, rhythmically tapping the fabric of the tent. My mind drifted back to Sheena's story about the older woman dying alone aboard the cruise with no one knowing who she was.

———

Nightmares consumed my sleep. I checked my bank account and saw that my balances were big fat zeros. A detective lounged in my apartment talking to me, trying to tell me about an arrest of a man who stole women's identities by pretending to be their boyfriend. Kurt . . . they arrested Kurt.

"We believe you were compromised and your identity stolen," he said.

No one needed to tell me that; my bank account revealed that truth. This wasn't a nightmare. It was a memory.

When I finally wrenched myself from sleep, it was light outside. The rain drizzled. The sound lulled my senses and my eyes grew heavy.

No! I forced myself to stay awake. Ellie and Sheena were passed out; one was lightly snoring. I checked my watch: 7:27 a.m. Reaching for my water bottle, I took several deep gulps.

My belly made a sloshing noise as I settled back. It was so full. I should have peed before bed but had dwelled too much on Sheena's story about the dead lady on the cruise. Someone would have identified her at some point. An elderly woman like that would have a family, wouldn't she? Also, when the coroner did a fingerprint or dental analysis, wouldn't that reveal who she was? There had to be some trace of her identity. No one had pulled out her teeth or shaved off her fingerprints. Someone would figure out who she was. I rubbed my hands on my face and then started to wring them. Ellie, being the ever-so-observant one—even when completely zonked out—woke up. Her face hovered over mine. She stroked my hair slowly and gently rubbed my shoulder.

"It's okay," she murmured. "You're here with us. You're safe."

73

The quaking of my heart eased, and my hands dropped to my side. "Do you want to talk about it?" she asked.

"It . . . it was Sheena's old woman. I wondered how someone could identify her with her dental records or fingerprints. Someone would have figured out who she is."

"Yes, I'm sure someone did," she sleepily agreed.

I rolled over to face her. "But what about me? How could someone identify me if I died? I'm in limbo right now. Are my dental records and fingerprints still associated with me even though I am desperately trying to get a new Social Security number?"

The warmth in Ellie's face subsided. "You're overreacting and worrying yourself into a dark place. Besides, we have a more dire situation to be worried about."

I rolled my eyes, eliciting a glare from her.

"Without reminding you, we are lost in the middle of the forest." She cleared her throat. "I've been doing a lot of research on your situation. You don't know if your identity has been used maliciously. Your lawyer helped you with the credit bureaus and the Social Security office to get things locked down and protected. Why jump the gun and fight them to give you a new identity? You run into a lot of difficulties going down that route. You'd be starting from square one all over again."

"Where do you think I am now? I have nothing right now, no money, and I am teetering on the edge of losing my apartment. I can't catch up and keep money in the bank because it is gone the moment a paycheck hits. All these lawyer fees have me in debt for the rest of my life. On top of that, I can't get a loan because my fucking credit is frozen." I raged, tears streaming down my face. Sheena's snoring had stopped. She was listening.

Ellie sat up. "Amelia, if you could stop thinking about yourself for one moment and realize that all three of us are up shit creek without a paddle right now, I would greatly appreciate it. Whining about your identity being stolen is nothing compared to what is going on now." She paused for a moment to cast a disgusted look at me. "We are lost in the middle of a fucking forest and have no idea how to get out."

I sat up and glared at her. "I know we are lost. But when we get home, you both have lives to return to. I don't. Researching the internet can't tell you how a person in this situation feels."

With that, I got up and put on my jeans, boots, and damp hiking jacket, ignoring Ellie's snotty comment: "If we get home." Sheena still said nothing and continued to lie there with eyes open, staring at the tent's roof. Ellie tried to get her to talk reason into me, but Sheena ignored her. *Good*, I thought; at least one of my friends understands.

I unzipped the tent, crawled into the rain, and zipped the tent back up. Once closed, Ellie snapped at Sheena, asking why she hadn't done anything to help.

"I am," Sheena said. "I am not telling her how to feel."

"Are you kidding me?" Ellie yelled and then, in a very hushed voice, said, "What if that little incident on the rocks was her trying to kill herself? Plus, she obviously doesn't care that the three of us are all in trouble right now, thanks to your overreliance on technology."

Suppressing the urge to yell "Fuck you," I flipped my hood over my head and stormed off into the forest—away from them.

The air was musky and damp. While my boots squished in the foliage debris that littered the ground, the canopy of a large oak tree provided some relief from the rain. Out of sight of the tent, I unzipped my pants, squatted, and stared into the forest as I relieved myself. The trees were slick and black, saturated by the steady hum of raindrops. A purplish-gray mist wove itself throughout the trees. The vast tree canopy above blocked out the morning sun. That's probably why there were no saplings or underbrush—insufficient sunlight for new growth.

This trip with Ellie and Sheena had been a good distraction for me—despite becoming lost. I had not thought about Kurt during the hike, at least not until my nightmare. But now that I was alone, I couldn't get him out of my mind. How could I not see the signs? Was I so blind? It was love. Love that was a farce, but I had allowed myself to be swept away by my emotions. Allowed myself to bend to his every whim. Dinners, movies, adventures—I'd paid for them all. I had thought it was because he was not as financially secure as I was. In reality, he had distracted me so that I didn't see what he was doing. Kurt used me and then stole from me. Now he has a well-fed life in jail for the next few years, while I don't have a penny to my name.

"Or a name at all," I whispered to myself.

I finished and stood, zipping up my pants. As I readjusted my sweater and pulled down my jacket, a whisper wove through the trees—scratchy and soft, harmonizing with the gentle, falling rain. A movement off to my left caught my eye. I saw something slide off a tree trunk and disappear around the other side. It was pale and fast.

"Hey!" I yelled out. My boots squished as I walked around the tree. Nothing was there. The whispering came again, this time to my right. I turned toward it, trying to pinpoint the sound. Another flash, and something skirted a different tree trunk. It moved like that little critter up on the mountain. It had to be a squirrel. No other animal moved like that. Back home, the squirrels were of the gray variety. These were pale. Maybe albino.

I continued to follow the whispering and flashes of movement. The rain let up, and the air warmed as fog arose from the balmy ground. I pushed my hood back and unzipped my jacket. The whispering amplified. The absence of rain made it easier to pinpoint it—directly in front of me now. Another pale flash around a tree trunk followed by an onslaught of whispering.

I stopped in my tracks and strained to listen. The whispering morphed into a sound like squirrels moving, their nails scratching on the bark as they ran up and down the trees.

I jumped as one whipped around a tree trunk before me, clinging motionless to the bark. It was long and thin. The animal remained frozen as I approached.

It wasn't a squirrel. It wasn't an animal but a human arm wrapped around the trunk. Grimacing, I wanted to look away but couldn't. The arm slipped back to the other side of the tree.

We were being followed this whole time. I swallowed rapidly.

All around me, arms wrapped around tree trunks, gripping hard at the bark with dirty, jagged fingernails connected to unseen bodies on the other side. The mist thickened, and I spun around and around, losing all sense of direction.

The whispering intensified, and the fingers began to dig into the bark, peeling away chunks and pieces so loudly that I could hear nothing else above it—except the whispers. I ran. In what direction, I didn't know. I ran to escape, but I couldn't get away from the arms. They haunted the forest. Ahead of me, every tree had an arm or two wrapped around its trunk, tearing away at the bark. As far as my eyes could see, the arms . . . were everywhere.

My knees buckled, and I hit the ground. Upon my impact, the arms shot around a tree and disappeared, leaving as the only evidence of their existence, the bark marred with scratches. The vacuum of silence returned. My chest fluttered as the thoughts of safety enveloped me, only to be instantly crushed. From behind a tree directly in front of me, a leg stepped out, unclothed, streaked with dirt. Behind the leg, a woman's body followed, naked and crusted in mud. Her head was slung low, and a tumble of black gnarled hair hung over her face. She walked toward me, her steps disjointed and abrupt, shoulders jerking with every slow step. The whispering returned, coming from her.

I pushed my legs into the ground, attempting to stand. My body wouldn't move. The whispering flooded my ears, drowning out all other sounds.

Now I knew what was being said. I fell under the spell of the words.

She stood next to me. A dirty hand that smelled of wet earth reached for my face, fingernails split and broken, caked with gray mud. Her head raised, hair falling away to reveal a clean, pristine, porcelain face. Empty. A blank slate, void of shape or purpose—a doll's face, waiting to be carved. Mystified, I didn't flinch when her hand shot forward, fingers clamping onto my face. Through her fingers, I stared at the blank canvas.

The moment she made contact, the skin under her face undulated as though there was an eel beneath, wriggling, trying to break free. A nose formed first, then the cheekbones, followed by eyebrows, lips, and a cleft chin. The gnarled black mess of her hair smoothed itself, becoming straight and blonde. Bones cracked as her height changed, hips realigned, and shoulders broadened. She leaned in, bringing her face closer to mine. Hollows grew in the space where her eyes should have been. I could not look away; I didn't want to look away. The hollows indented more, then bubbled out. When the bubbles reached their limit, they split perfectly horizontally, dripping a greenish ooze. As the skin separated, white orbs appeared then rotated, bringing forth two irises. My vision became hazy as she looked at me with her new eyes. Her green eyes stared deeply into my green ones—the last things I saw before the world went black.

The cool, damp earth cushioned my body as I fell. Her whispers continued to drum in my head, beating louder and louder. When the whispers reached the loudest, the spell broke and I felt free.

My hands reached for my face, tracing my features, but I felt nothing distinguishable: no lips, no nose, no eyes, no ears. The ability to talk, to breathe, or to hear is lost, but how my body feels right now, I'll never need to do any of those things again. My senses are dead in this new, dark world. The only comfort I have now is the woman's whispers, repeating inside my head: "I am Amelia; I am Amelia."

The Voiceless

Maria came home today. The bruising around her right eye is a sickly greenish purple. The hospital left the bandages wrapped around her neck. It's for the better. The bandages hide the true damage. She shouldn't be here. She shouldn't have returned.

He walks in behind her, carrying her red and white–striped overnight bag, smiling like a happy crocodile. The lock clicks the moment he shuts the door, and his smile grows even larger as he puts the key in his pocket. Maria doesn't know that he changed the locks while she was away; now a key is needed to get out.

It was never like that when I was the only one here with him.

He drops Maria's bag and walks past it, past her, past me into the living room. Neither acknowledges me; then again, they never do. Maria looks at the clock on the wall. It's a little after noon. Her shoulders rise and fall as she takes in a breath and silently lets out a sigh.

I follow her as she walks into the kitchen. Standing next to the sink she carefully pulls a dish from the cupboard and a knife from the drawer, cautious not to make any clatter. He's in the living room, watching television. He hates any noise that pulls him away from the fantasy world playing out on the screen. From the refrigerator, she retrieves Lebanon bologna, two yellow American cheese slices that are individually wrapped in plastic, and a jar of mayonnaise that I believe is long expired. Maria places everything on the kitchen counter next to the dish in order of assembly.

She fishes out two slices of white bread and sets them side by side on the dish. A hand goes up to the side of her face, and she pushes her curly mousy brown hair behind her multi-pierced ear. She has six studs and one hoop in her left ear and two hoops and three studs in her right. I don't understand why she has so many piercings or the reasoning behind the lack of symmetry. There is a small outline of a heart tattooed on the inside of her left wrist with an "R" in the center of it. A tribute to her young son, Ricki, who was abducted from her nearly six years ago and is believed to be dead despite his body never being found. I wish she'd never moved here to this haunted town, Deimos. She was safer on the seashores of Maine.

Maria stares at the two slices of bread on the plate. Her mouth starts to move, and whispers come out. The words are scratchy, and I can't make out what she's saying. I don't think she is praying. She never prays. Maria doesn't notice me get closer as I lean in to hear her words. Whatever she is saying sounds like static on the radio to me. She looks in my direction and I stand up straight, trying to hide that I was eavesdropping in case she saw me. She looks past me toward the window above the sink. Her brown eyes are glassy with tears.

Her hand clenches around a knife, and her focus returns to the task at hand. With the knife, she scoops mayonnaise out of the jar and slathers it on both slices of bread. She spreads on so much there are waves of creamy white rolling across the bread's surface, boiling like the sea. He loves mayonnaise. She uses my old chef's knife to lather the bread, and I don't know why she chose a big sharp knife over a butter knife. She isn't in her right mind right now, so she probably wasn't paying attention.

The individual slices of cheese are removed from the plastic wrapping and set gently on the sea of mayonnaise washing over each bread slice. Three pieces of Lebanon bologna go on the left slice of bread, spread out like a Venn diagram. Maria closes the sandwich by laying the right bread slice, cheese side down, on top of the Lebanon bologna. She has made the sandwich exactly the way he likes it. Before she takes the sandwich to him in the living room, she stops at the refrigerator and pulls out two cans of beer.

He will be pleased.

———

We had a history once, he and I. It started off wonderful and full of brilliance. It was love, or what I thought was love. Unfortunately, I was too young and naive as a recent graduate from Deimos High; he was older and more experienced as my twelfth-grade math teacher. I lived in his world and by his rules. He proposed marriage to me on a gloomy April day, using the promise of college to entice my agreement. My family could not afford to send me to school, but he said he could. I readily agreed because I loved him and wanted to go to college.

This house was originally our home together, and I maintained it impeccably. My role in our relationship was to keep house while he continued to teach, which sustained a roof over our heads. He'd come home at 5:30 p.m. on the dot every day with freshly picked flowers for me in spring and summer. When flowers were dead in fall and winter, he would find little trinkets or stones for me. Over meals together we'd talk of topics in the realm of physics and theory for him, history and literature for me. These were his ways of showing I was appreciated. In return, I made a home for him.

The world was right; our marriage was perfect for the first two years. Then one day he came home with the idea of starting a family.

I wasn't so sure if I wanted that yet. I'd just turned twenty and was still waiting for my chance to go to college. He asked me to put that on hold to have a child. It would make our family complete, and he could achieve his dream. Then I would be able to achieve mine.

———

Maria returns to the kitchen to clean up. I heard no words pass between them when she gave him his sandwich. The only sound coming from the living room is violence from what I was sure was *Rambo*, his favorite movie.

I am still standing next to the sink in the kitchen, watching her as she sweeps up the crumbs and puts away the sandwich items. She still does not acknowledge me, even though I've been standing within feet of her this whole time. This is normal.

She uses the blue and white–checkered dish towel to wipe the mayonnaise off my chef's knife. I cringe as she puts the dishtowel back where she grabbed it off the handle of the broken dishwasher. She didn't rinse the cloth out.

Instead of placing the knife in the sink, she holds it against her thigh as she walks out of the kitchen, past the living room, and into the foyer. He doesn't look away from the television as she passes. I follow her out, curious as to what she is doing. Maria picks her bag off the foyer floor, shouldering it with a grimace, and makes her way upstairs to the bedroom. The stairs creak with each step she takes. This house is growing old.

A loud *rat-tat-tat* of gunfire draws my attention, and I walk over to him in the living room, my emotions brimming on the edge of annoyance. Maria was gone for nearly a week, and he hasn't spoken a word to her since she returned.

A door upstairs closes. He disgusts me. The shirt he has on is three days old. There was a small hole once in the armpit of the shirt, but it's grown to the size of a half-dollar. Long black hairs poke through the hole when he raises his arm above his head. His jeans have never been washed. There is always a sickly smell of body odor on them. His face is constantly grizzled. His expectation for his house was that his woman would take care of everything. He no longer looks or acts like a scholar.

Since I can no longer care for him or the house, it is now Maria's responsibility.

———

College never came, neither did the baby.

We found out that we were pregnant on a rainy afternoon in August. He was elated. I sat with a smile on my face while the doctor told us the news. Deep down, I didn't feel like this was what I wanted. But he did. If I gave him that, I'd eventually get what I wanted.

Once I accepted my reality, I eventually fell in love with my baby girl. My doctor said it was still too early to tell what the gender was, but I knew she was a girl. A mother knows. I would sing to her all day and talk to her at night before going to bed. It would annoy him, and he would say awful things to me to make me shut up. He thought it was stupid to talk to something growing inside of me that he could not tangibly see. From then on, I would only speak and sing to her when he was away. She could hear me; I knew it.

Despite being pregnant, he expected me to continue keeping the house in tip-top condition. I was terribly ill during the first trimester, but I somehow found the energy to clean and make him three meals daily.

One week I must have overdone it because I'd gotten my period. It was noticeably light, and when I called the doctor's office about it, they said for me to go on bed rest until next week, when they could fit me in for an ultrasound. However, if the bleeding became any heavier, I needed to go to the ER immediately.

———

He wolfs down the sandwich, oblivious that I'm standing right next to him. Above our heads, I can hear the splash of water filling the tub. Maria is in the bathroom. I leave him and make my way upstairs. The stairs no longer creak when I walk up them. Maria doesn't hear me enter the bathroom. Her back is to me in the tub. A gentle stream swirls from the faucet, filling the tub with warm, soothing water. It's comforting in here despite the room not being thoroughly cleaned since I was last in the tub. Black mold grows around the base and up the corner of the walls. The toilet has eternal grime clinging to the porcelain. The paint from the wall is peeling and curling because he never installed an exhaust fan like he was supposed to or fixed the window so that it could be opened to vent the room.

I hate what this house has become since I haven't been able to care for it. To give Maria credit, she does try, but she cares less than I did. I believe it's because he made no promises to her other than to provide a roof over her head. Maria doesn't have dreams like I used to, like how I once wanted to go to college and become an author. And then, when the pregnancy situation was forced upon me, how my dream changed to being a mother. Maria seems to coast by with him, giving him only what he needs and never going beyond. That is what I'm sure fuels his anger toward her, the fact that she puts in just enough effort to care for him and nothing more.

Sitting on the toilet behind the tub, I watch her gently slide her hands up and down her damaged neck. Maria went through all of that and returned, slipping right back into her role of caring for him. I am not sure if she is displaying weakness . . . or pragmatism.

Maybe just having a roof over her head is Maria's only dream. I place my head in my hands. I remember once hearing that she lived in a shelter before meeting him. Maybe she was just going to put enough energy into her situation in order to stay. However, given her recent hospital visit, I believe she would fight to maintain her place here. She would fight for what she wanted, unlike me.

I am the weak one.

———

On the Saturday after the bleeding started, I awoke in extreme pain. I knew something was wrong with the baby. The doctor's words hadn't been heeded, but it was because I wasn't allowed rest. That morning I mowed the lawn with our battered push mower. He told me to mow because he had a hard week at work and needed to relax.

While I was lying in bed that night, the convulsions in my abdomen started. Then there was an odd twinge and a gush between my legs. I ran to the bathroom, blood trickling down my legs. When I pulled down my underwear, I saw her lying there on the pad. She was so tiny, about the size of a prune.

He woke up when I ran from the bedroom and barged into the bathroom after me. Anger flushed across his face when he saw me, tear-streaked and holding our expelled child in my hand. His face contorted into something monstrous, and the backhand across my face knocked me into the tub. He grabbed the front of my nightdress and slammed me back against the porcelain, again and again. My vision darkened as he stepped away, and I struggled to understand what was going on. I heard the toilet flush. The rushing sound of water roared in my ears. My baby wasn't in my hand. Everything around me became wet and freezing. He held me down, pushing his weight onto my chest. I could not figure out what he was doing until I felt the water rising.

I tried to kick and punch, but he had me wedged in the tub, pinned down by his body weight. The water continued to rise.

"Please, let's try again," I pleaded. His black and hollow eyes bored into my own. The water splashed at the corners of my lips. Grabbing his forearms, I tried to pry him off my shoulders.

"We could even adopt." I sputtered on the last word as the water seeped in past my lips. "Please!" I choked and tried to thrash my way out from beneath his hands. Nothing I said snapped him out of the grotesque trance he was in. He just stared at me with those hate-filled eyes. I'd lost his child. My body was defective.

The water was too high. Pushing my nose above the surface, I drew in a deep breath before the water, tinged red with my blood, engulfed my head. I kept my eyes open, staring at his face. He didn't allow me to hold onto my last breath long as he leaned his forearms away from my shoulder and pushed them down on my chest, expelling the remaining air from my lungs.

———

He found Maria after he silenced me because he needed someone else to manage the house when I could no longer do so. Upon seeing Maria for the first time, I knew she was not as meticulous as I was, and she is often the brunt of his anger. At first he started yelling at her when she messed up. Afterward, she would run to the bathroom, lock herself in, and cry. I would always go in and try to speak to her about what she needed to do differently. She never seemed to hear me.

Friends would call to check in on her, and she regaled them with a fantasy life where she lived happily. She lied to them about how he'd whisk her away to travel the world, never being home long, dissuading anyone from visiting. She convinced them that her dreams had come true.

At first I hated her for taking my place, but soon that feeling turned into hating her for staying and being subject to him. My pleas to her to escape continued to go unheard. Maria will never leave this house and will do anything to ensure she has a place to live, even if the situation is not safe.

Her life with him is much bleaker than mine. After me, he grew darker and more hateful. Then came the moment when he'd had his fill of her, just as he'd finally had of me.

He tried to silence her last week in the kitchen for dropping a dish. He punched her in the face. When she fell, she started to scream terrible things at him, things that I could never bring myself to say or even think. Without any warning, he was on top of her with his hands around her throat. She looked toward where I stood next to the stove. Her eyes became dimmer, and my skin tingled. She was becoming like me, but I didn't want her to. I grew hot. I felt as though I'd stuck my finger in a light socket—that I would explode. Anger. I was infused with anger because I didn't think I could physically stop what was happening to her. My arm flailed out and hit the pot of water on the stove that Maria was going to boil for spaghetti.

The pot crashed to the floor, spilling water everywhere. He jumped off her while she writhed on the floor, trying to catch her breath. There was a popping sound when she breathed. He stared dumbly at the pot on the floor then at the stove then back to the pot, his face filled with confusion and terror. In that moment, I think he acknowledged that he had almost created another "me" and took her to the hospital. I don't know how he was able to get around the situation without being charged with domestic abuse, but he'd gotten away with it once. He'd gotten away with much more before.

———

I move and sit next to the tub to watch her. The bandages around her neck are gone, revealing deep purple bruises dotted with finger marks. Her head is back against a folded towel, eyes closed, and she is again moving her mouth, trying to speak. I still cannot understand her whispers. He crushed her larynx. It may or may not heal.

Something metal scrapes the bottom of the tub. Her arms are at her side. Looking into the tub, I see she has my chef's knife in her left hand. Terror seizes me. This is not the escape I want for her. She can't do this. If she does, she'll become like me, trapped in this house, invisible for all of eternity. No one will ever see her again, just as no one has seen me since the night he drowned me in this tub.

I reach for the knife, but my hand goes right through. She shivers when I make contact and opens her eyes. The feeling of electricity sizzles through my body. I try again, and this time I knock the knife from her hand. It falls to the bottom of the bathtub with a metallic thud. We look at each other, but I am sure she cannot see me. She continues to whisper words I don't quite catch. I hear the scrape of the knife again as she picks it back up. I plead with her to stop, to not do this. I tell her to go get dressed, pack her red and white–striped bag, and run away. Sneak out the bedroom window. Run away like I should have when I first saw his oppressiveness.

Over and over I scream at her to escape, to not become trapped here in this horrible house like me. Maria raises her arms out of the water, knife in her right hand. I can't watch what she does next and turn away from her. I focus on her whispers, it's the only thing I can do to distract myself from what she is about to do.

"Ricki." Her whispers are now clear. She is calling to her lost little boy. "Please, Ricki; I don't want to be alone anymore. Come find Mommy."

She lifts the blade of the knife to her left wrist. I summon my strength and knock the knife from her hand again. It clatters off the edge of the tub and onto the cracked tiled floor. We both stare at it. Between us the air pulsates with warmth. Of understanding. She doesn't reach for the knife.

Maria stands, pulls the drain plug, and watches the water disappear. Once gone, she steps out of the tub, picks up the knife, and walks out of the bathroom, naked and dripping wet.

As I follow down the stairs, each step she takes creaks. In the living room, his attention is still fully on the television, but he knows she's just entered the room. He holds an empty beer can above his head and shakes it, indicating that he wants a fresh can.

The sound in the room amplifies. His saggy, wheezing breath crackles in unison with the hissing static of the television's suddenly poor reception. The skin of Maria's hand rubs a low fleshy squeak as she grips the knife's wooden handle. Naked feet wetly squish on the shag carpet she walks up behind him. The beer can flies out of his hand—struck by her open hand—and hits the wall with a tinny gong. As soon as the contact is made, he looks up at her, anger flushing his face. She moves so quickly that he doesn't immediately register that she's stabbing him in the neck and face. He tries to get away, but the force of her attack holds his body down on his favorite tan recliner that turns crimson with his blood.

Sentence should read as:

Maria turns off the television and staggers back, falling onto the sofa. She shivers and pulls the blanket from the back of the sofa across her body, covering her nakedness. I sit down next to her, and we stare at his body as it spasms. Once it goes still, I look around the room, expecting to see him. I don't. He's gone. He's not trapped here like me.

Maria breathes in and then exhales a long breath. She touches a fingertip to the small tattoo on her left wrist in tribute to her lost son. Her trembling lips stretch into a crooked smile louder than any words she'll ever speak again.

Carrion Eaters

If Daddy were here right now, he'd be madder than heck at the trail of blood leading from the house's decaying front porch to the middle of the sandy dirt road. He'd probably argue with Mama about it, saying that it'd reveal which house we were hiding in, but Mama would say not to worry because the Carrion Eaters only feast on the dead.

From what they'd revealed to me, Brandon and Seth didn't like the situation either. But that didn't keep them from wrapping the body lying in the dining room up in the old blue patchwork quilt like Mama asked them to. Then they dragged it outside.

"Leave 'em right in the middle of the road within direct sight of the upstairs right window," Mama hollers at them.

I tend not to listen to her. We never got along, with me being unplanned and just another mouth to feed. Probably why I ended up being a daddy's girl. But he's not here, so I reluctantly do as I'm told.

"Lily, you git that blood in the dining room and front hall cleaned up. And do it right quick," she snaps. She carries her rifle up the rickety old staircase, her footsteps thudding across the second floor, shaking dust loose to rain down on me. The scraping drag of the armchair across the floor indicates that she's set her sight out the right window of the front bedroom.

The puddle in the dining room and the streak leading to the front door are thin, and some areas are drying. The hinges of the closet creak as I fetch the pail and mop. Leaving the mop near the blood, I traipse out the back of the house, pail in hand, to extract water from the rusty hand pump standing among the calf-high prairie grass. The pump's handle is warm from sitting beneath a clear-day sun, and it squawks like a strangled bird as sulfur-stained water sputters from the nozzle while I vigorously pump the handle as though shaking the hand of a good friend I hadn't seen in years.

My fingers slip from the pump as I think about lost friends. It's been over a year since my family has seen another person. The last person we saw wasn't even a friend. We don't know who he was, but he broke into our home. And Daddy and Seth attacked the man while Brandon pulled me and Mama away. The attack ended with Daddy's nose bloodied then Seth stabbing the stranger in the neck. All would have been well if not for a kerosene lamp that had been pitched into the plaster wall, just below the sitting room window. Flames licked and caught Mama's crochet curtains on fire, sending flaming fingers across the room.

My family's entire life burnt down that night. We salvaged what we could before going off in search of a new place to live and thrive, which is how we ended up in this new house. But we aren't thriving, and we don't have any food. This afternoon we ate our last meal together as a family when we finished off a tin of beans.

I finish pumping the water and turn back to the house.

A few other houses are situated nearby, all vacant and hollow, each having its own barn that used to house livestock, and each equally decrepit. A sparse copse of gangly trees surround these houses, which is odd to see in the middle of a prairie. Daddy said it was because there is a lot of water underground, which may be why they built homes here. I like to think of it as an underground lake, and we are all just floating on the surface. Only Daddy ever found that thought interesting.

This house floating on the underground lake is small, though, and it's starting to decay. But it has a metal roof—which is rare for these parts due to the expense. Daddy once said a roof like this was good for long-term durability. We've only been hiding in the house for six months, so I can't speak to that yet.

"Immaculate," Daddy called our home. This place isn't that. At our old home, we lived well off the land, with annual gardens full of vegetables that were canned along with fruits for the cold seasons. The canned goods always lasted us through the winter. Daddy and I expanded the garden to grow pumpkins and squash in that final spring. It flourished well—such a bounty of food.

Though, as much as I enjoy eating of the earth, I miss the taste of meat.

Two years ago we woke one morning to find all the animals dead—and not just those on our farm. Yes, the few cows and chickens we owned lay dead in or around the barn. But the corpses of all sorts of animals littered the prairie—from birds to deer, little gophers to frogs, grasshoppers, and butterflies, seemingly all dead. Not even the flies survived.

Rumors came from the closest town, Yellow Creek City, that the deaths were widespread across the state; some believed, possibly the country. It wasn't just us. And everyone was just as perplexed as to what had happened. Some folks took a chance to save some of the recently deceased meat, while others—like my family—burned all the corpses we came across because Daddy believed they carried a sickness. He didn't want any of us to catch it.

The mass deaths coincided with the arrival of the Carrion Eaters. I was the first to see them—smell them, actually. Their musty, decaying scent wafted on the prairie breeze; it was hard to miss. I'd been out collecting tubers but eventually grew bored of digging up the weeds and began to wander around the prairie, missing the sound of chirping birds and staring off into the cloudy blue sky, imagining the clouds shifting into the shapes of the missing wildlife. That's when I caught wind and saw three of them hunched over the corpse of a large buck not even thirty feet away from me. At first I had thought them to be massive vultures and got excited over seeing a living bird. I squealed out of sheer joy. At the sound, the black haunches of the birds had expanded and unfurled, revealing they were not vultures at all.

They stood taller than Daddy, on four long spindly legs. Shaggy black, gnarled fur hung in curtains from tailless, seemingly emaciated bodies. With their rear legs being shorter than their front, their backs had heaved like hunched vultures, which is what caused the mistaken identity.

Snarls and chortles had mingled with the sound of tearing meat and cracking bone as they returned to their consumption of the carcass that lay between them. Their pristine white and skinless skulls were streaked red up to the two small racks of antlers that sat just above their eyeless sockets. As no flesh covered their heads, I could clearly see their molars behind long sharp canines slowly grinding away at the carrion they fed upon.

Fear had rooted me where I stood. If I hadn't been so scared, I would have wondered how they kept the rancid meat in their mouths.

My fingers had twitched as the urge to run flooded my senses and the basket, filled with tubers, fell from my grasp to land with a soft thud. This time the sound I made got their full attention. The heads of all three monsters snapped up in unison to stare at me. How terrible to be caught in that empty stare, those orbless eyes. I tensed up, ready for them to attack, but they just turned heel and rambled off across the prairie, running like a pack of stiff-legged deer.

As they departed, fear turned my own feet toward the house and my family.

No one believed me for several days. Not until Brandon came home with his face white as a ghost's.

"There's one in the barn," he'd whispered.

Daddy and Seth grabbed their guns and ran out of the house toward the barn. Before they reached the building, the beast ran through the doors Brandon had left open and took off like a scared little fawn.

From that day forward, seeing the creatures on the grasslands became a regular occurrence as they picked clean the animal corpses scattered about the land. Daddy and my brothers, from their trading trips to Yellow Creek City, brought home stories about townsfolk who'd seen them too. Some folks even claimed to have hunted and eaten the beasts, though Daddy said we wouldn't be doing that. In fact, we planned to let them be, as they weren't harming us. Who knew what kind of sicknesses they might carry from eating all those animal corpses? Besides, there didn't seem to be any meat to them.

Mama and he fought often about that. When we were kids, we never saw our parents argue. We'd hear them sometimes at night when we were tucked away in the darkness of our bedrooms, but they never quarreled in front of us. Until that day. From that point forward, Mama constantly picked fights with Daddy, telling him he was wrong, and that he was starving his children. While Brandon and Seth agreed with her, when out of ear shot, they claimed they agreed with Daddy.

We'd done well in that home for many years in this new animal-free world, just living off what we could grow or trade. Often it wasn't enough because we'd still be left hungry.

Folks in Yellow Creek City had been surviving just like us until they started turning against one another. We were too far out of town to be affected, but Daddy and my brothers came back with the news from the last trading trip—everyone in Yellow Creek had done killed one another.

An argument between Mama and Daddy the next day drove the final wedge between them.

Daddy gathered us around the dining room table for a family discussion.

"After the great flood, God's children were permitted to eat meat," Daddy said and bowed his head as he quoted Genesis 9:3. *Every moving thing that lives shall be food for you, And as I gave you the green plants, I give you everything.*

The boys nodded. Mama glared at Daddy while I looked on in confusion.

He cleared his throat. "Yesterday, when me and the boys were in town, we had to kill the Patson brothers."

I gasped at the thought of my daddy hurting—let alone killing—another person. My brothers, maybe, but never Daddy.

Mama had no reaction.

"They had a larder of townsfolk in their home," his voice cracked. "They had killed and were eating everyone."

"If we didn't hurt them, they would've hurt us," Seth said, leaning back in his chair and crossing his arms over his chest. Brandon looked down at the table, saying nothing.

"What drove them to do that?" I whispered.

"They were scavenging the dead animals before moving on to people," Seth said, glaring at me. "Eating the animal meat probably made them sick. That's why Daddy told us not to do it."

Daddy smiled at Seth.

"You tell us not to kill, yet you killed," Mama murmured.

"These are strange times," Daddy said, ignoring her. "I don't know what our future will become, but this family will survive." He pounded his fist on the table.

"Of course we will," said Brandon.

"We'll outlast them all," said Seth.

Daddy continued. "There are rules we as a family need to follow to keep safe."

Mama scoffed and rolled her eyes.

"We grow our own food and protect this house," Daddy said, and the boys agreed.

Mama said nothing.

"Second, we eat no meat. We go back to God's original diet for us. We eat only what grows from the land." He slid his chair back and stood. "No one in this household will eat the animal carcasses or the carrion-eating beasts. And no one will eat another human being."

The boys nodded their heads while Mama's face turned a deep red. "We can't survive on plants alone!" she snapped at him.

"We can and will. There is no debating this. To do anything else is blasphemy."

"Blasphemy? How is this blasphemy?" she screamed at him.

"God killed all the animals of this planet, leaving his children to eat only what grows from the land," Daddy said.

"And what about those beasts?" she snapped.

"God sent them here to consume those carcasses. He will take them back once they've cleaned the land."

"You have an answer for everything," Mama said.

"There is no other explanation." Daddy slammed his fist once more on the table.

Mama slid her chair back and stormed out of the house. But before she left, she turned to glare at my daddy and brothers—who had sided against her. For once, she didn't cast her anger at me.

Daddy's rules of living off the land would probably have worked well if we could have lived in our house forever with our established garden and fresh well water. But Mama forgot to lock the door after she returned home. A locked door may have prevented that stranger from sneaking into our home and attacking us, which ultimately led to our home being burnt down.

This place where we live now, built by the hands of another family, isn't home with its slatted and drafty wooden walls, creaky floorboards, and tattered furniture covered with dust. We've not been doing well in making do, as we were never able to reproduce our grand garden on this land.

The past few weeks have become more grueling than ever since Mama increased the food rationing. We've all taken on the gaunt, hollow look the Carrion Eaters initially had when they arrived. However, as we grew thinner, the beasts grew fatter. We cannot figure out what the beasts are eating to remain so plump—all that's left of the long-dead animals are bits of sun-leathered skin and weathered skeletons; yet the Carrion Eaters roam the prairies with full bellies.

"Lily, we can't keep going on like this." Mama sounded exhausted as we sat next to each other on the front porch floor. A small herd of the beasts migrated down the sandy dirt road in front of the house. They pass by without even a glance in our direction. They don't care about the living.

"Daddy says we'll survive," I said.

"Your daddy will kill us all." Mama watched the Carrion Eaters walk away from us. "We're done with his rules. It's time to stop letting those beasts be."

I gasped, "But Daddy says—"

"To hell with what your daddy says," she declared.

The argument she had with Daddy was brief, as he'd grown tired over these past couple of months. The fire that used to burn strongly within him had waned, and he looked sickly. Daddy had not been eating his full share of rations and was sharing his food with me out of sight of Mama and my brothers.

Seth and Brandon took me outside while Daddy and Mama talked. Brandon sang a song about a woman named Clementine to drown out whatever our parents were saying.

Mama called us into the house and said it was time to eat. We went to the dining room where a tattered blue patchwork quilt lay spread across the floor, serving as our dining room table. Over the winter, Daddy and my brothers had chopped up the actual dining room table for firewood. Right in the center of the quilt was an open tin of beans with a fork stuck inside.

"There's enough for everyone to have a bite." She clenched the hem of her faded rose skirt sideways as she sat on the floor. Beside her lay a rifle. Daddy was the first to pick up the can of beans, and without taking a forkful, he handed the tin to me.

"You can have my share," he said. Tears brimmed in his distant-looking eyes.

Seth went to say something, but Brandon elbowed him.

I put a forkful in my mouth and so fully lost myself in the soft feel of the beans that I had not realized I'd taken my second bite. Seth ripped the tin from my hand and shoveled his portion in his mouth before passing along the tin. Once my brothers and Mama had their share, Mama set the tin aside and then pulled five straws, taken from the house broom, from the pocket of her skirt.

"There is something special one of us must do today." She fumbled with the straws before looking at Seth and Brandon. "The one who draws the shortest straw has a job to do. They are going to sacrifice themselves for the family."

I had been the only one to gasp, and I looked wildly at the faces of my family. No one else reacted. My brothers and father stared at the tablecloth.

"The one who is sacrificed will be wrapped up in my quilt"—she lovingly stroked the fabric before her—"then taken out to the road in front of the house and left there to lure in the Carrion Eaters. We're going to kill one of the beasts." Her hands shook. "We need food," she shouted before drawing the first straw, followed by Brandon then Seth. They all had the same lengths and were safe.

Mama breathed a sigh that sounded of relief, then leaned forward, thrusting her fist with two straws sticking up before us. Daddy pulls both straws at the same time—mine and his.

I'd never seen Mama raise a rifle and pull the trigger so fast.

The Wreckage of Sin

The woman's mouth formed a perfect pink "O" as her body connected with the hood of Bailey's car. Long blonde hair splayed across the windshield—a splash of red tainting the color of the golden sun. Bailey couldn't see the pickup truck in front of her. The woman separated the front of Bailey's car from the back of the truck owned by a lanky farmer.

Bailey couldn't recall the woman's eyes, but she'd never forget the farmer's. Hate sullied them as he held the woman's hand, talking to her, soothing words filtering through the cracked windshield. Someone opened Bailey's door and pushed away the deployed airbag. An empty bottle of tequila fell out, shattering on the street. She'd just come from another failed audition. Still not skinny enough.

"She's drunk!" A voice screamed.

"Call 9-1-1," said another.

"This girl . . . ," said the farmer, his voice hollow as he held the woman's wrist. "She's dead."

———

A rhythmic beeping to Bailey's left indicated that she was still alive. A perfect sinus rhythm. She tapped her middle finger to the beat. The rhythm's cadence increased when her heart rate spiked as the first sensation of pain lanced through her body. The agonizing scream that tore from her throat signaled nearby nurses. Their voices melded together as the painkillers set in.

———

"Every action has an equal and opposite reaction." A woman sat with her back to Bailey and beside her right leg, suspended in traction. The woman's long hair glowed as if it were the rays of the sun.

"What?" Bailey's voice cracked through parched lips. She blinked; the woman was gone.

"I hope you learned a valuable lesson," a man said. Bailey turned her head to the left in surprise and saw a haggard Doctor Hargrave standing next to her; salt-and-pepper hair extended from his head to his face, where a two-day-old beard sprouted. Eyes heavy with the need for sleep, he flipped through a chart and checked the electrodes adhered to her body, the numbers on the screen letting everyone know she was still alive.

"You've got a long road ahead of you." The doctor snapped the folder shut and walked around the bed to inspect her broken leg. Hargrave's hands were cold as he unraveled the gauze. A dark red, sutured line mapped out Bailey's greatest mistake from her knee to hip. The long road ahead of her was not just physical therapy. It was court, jail time, physical rehab, and living her life knowing she was a murderer.

On top of that, her modeling career was over. Her legs went on for days, perfectly shaped and toned. Who would hire her now with this disgusting scar? Bailey could never again boast that her gams were flawless.

But what kind of modeling career did she have anyway? Her agent rarely found her work, and when he did she was portrayed in ads for cookware or shoes. Posing with muffin tins wasn't her dream. She wanted to be an Angel. But she was a size 6 and an A cup. Too big in the hips, too small in the chest. Her agent told her that cosmetic work needed to be done to get her the contracts she wanted. He must have given her twenty business cards to plastic surgeons up and down the East Coast.

If she did what he told her, she'd have a chance to be something more. Yet she'd be altered. Enhanced. Not all her body parts would be her own. Would she still be herself in the end?

She should have stayed the course of being the woman her mother wanted her to be. One who'd marry young, make a loving house for a husband, and bear the grandchildren her mother longed for.

You're letting the devil corrupt your eyes, her mother would say whenever she'd see Bailey fuss over her appearance. *It's a sin to be so vain and disrespect the body that God gave you.*

But hadn't God gifted humans with free will? Giving her the right to choose what *she* wanted for *her* body? No one owned her body but her.

Yet Bailey understood that to make it in the beauty industry, she needed to meet its standards. And those standards caused her to obsess over how she wasn't good enough in this current form. Magazines only printed women with the perfect hourglass shape. No stretch marks lined their inner thighs; no scars marred their faces; no yellow-stained, crooked teeth tarnished their smiles. The most successful models were as perfect-looking as a Barbie doll.

Relentless thoughts of scalpels and stitches haunted her. She toiled in a sea that tossed her body among waves of opinions: to be natural or conform; to achieve a dream or let it go; to sin or not—

"Yeowch!!" Bailey screeched.

Hot electricity shot up her leg and spine as Hargrave probed at the leg wound. "Can't let you get infected. We can't let you suffer. Not now, at least."

"Ow!" Bailey yelled again as Hargrave moved to her face, prodding the bone under her eye. Her right side had taken the brunt of the accident. She'd had her leg straight and locked, pushing the gas pedal to the floor. Before Hargrave had entered her room, outside the open door, whispers swirled about suicide. Bailey was sure the crash wasn't suicidal and that she hadn't intentionally locked her leg. No, she was just plain old sad. Sad enough to allow alcohol to take control of her life.

"The force of the impact to the back of the truck snapped your femur. One of the strongest bones in the body snapped in half like a twig. The airbag pushed you back in the seat, but since you weren't wearing your seatbelt and were sitting too close to the dashboard," Hargrave said, "you bounced off the seat and smashed your face into the steering wheel. The airbag deflated too quickly to catch you, and now your lower-right eye socket is partially shattered." Bailey swore she saw a slight smile twitch the corner of his lips.

"Am I disfigured?" She tried to hide the tremble in her voice.

"You're alive and not in jail . . . yet."

Hargrave left, walking around the sheet that separated her from the empty bed beside her. She heard the door shut and exhaled with relief that the prodding and poking was over. The doctor was rougher than he should have been. Pain intensified throughout her body from the exam. She closed her eyes and started to fade into sleep when footsteps approached. She opened her eyes to see the doctor standing at the foot of the bed, hands wrapped around the top of the footboard. Hate, so reminiscent of the farmer, glinted in his eyes as he stared down at Bailey, who shifted uncomfortably in the bed.

"She was one of us," Hargrave said. Only his lips moved. The man was rigid as a statue.

"I'm sorry, who?" Bailey asked, wetting her lips as she focused on hiding the tremors that rattled her body.

"The woman you killed. Maise Blatt. She was a nurse here—one of my best nurses."

The tremors, now visible, moved up and down her arms. She raised a hand and placed it over her uninjured eye; hot tears streamed down her face. "I'm sorry. I'm so sorry."

"She didn't deserve what you did to her. Maise had a traumatic life." He ground his hands back and forth on the footboard so tightly that vibrations thrummed the mattress. "When she was a little girl, her mother was murdered. Her father claimed Maise did it and that she tried to kill him too. He had her shipped off to the psychiatric hospital on the other side of town. God knows what happened to her there. It's a miracle that she turned out to be the incredible soul she is," he coughed and glared at Bailey. "Was."

She looked away from him and tried to push down the rising bubble of tears and screams that heaved in her chest.

Hargrave walked to Bailey's injured side and caressed her exposed leg wound. He redressed it with a package of sterile gauze he had brought in. Her right cheek burned from crying, and she looked at the doctor through her fingers. A thin smile traced Hargrave's lip.

"It's okay. I made things right."

"What do you mean?" Bailey whispered.

"Your sin will stay with you for the rest of your life. Long after you're dead."

"I don't . . . I don't understand."

Hargrave caressed her gauze-wrapped thigh; a thin smile that looked like admiration for his work stretched across his face. "What

MADNESS AND GREATNESS can Share the Same face

you did is now part of you." He touched Bailey's thigh again and nodded toward her face. She placed her fingertips upon the wound on her cheek. The bones underneath the flesh were now held together with metal. The same with her shattered femur, once more made whole with metal. With metal . . . The sound of the front end of her car smashing into the back of the old pickup truck. The scraping screech of the metal. Blonde hair, like the sun's rays, splayed across her blood-splattered windshield. The pink, perfect "O" formed lips.

"My bones . . ." Her voice squeaked, and she couldn't bring herself to ask.

Hargrave's smile spread; brilliant white teeth sparkled. "Oh, yes; your little accident is a part of you."

Bailey squinted her eyes in confusion.

"Maybe I had my brother, a welder, make some adjustments to the metal plates and pins now holding your bones together by using metal from the truck's bumper you crashed into."

Bile rose in Bailey's mouth. "You're lying," she said. "You can't get away with that today."

"Or maybe," Hargrave continued, ignoring her, "your bone and skin graphs are a donation from my friend that you murdered."

A pit formed in her stomach, and she prayed it would expand, swallowing her whole before her curiosity overtook her fear and horror. "Which one did you do?"

Hargrave leaned in close; his sickly-sweet breath swept across Bailey's face, making her gag. "You'll never know.

———

Bailey welcomed the pain that bled through her all night, not once calling a nurse to administer morphine. She not only wanted to avoid them but also needed to live with the pain as her punishment. She

105

couldn't sleep but would fake it when someone came in to check her vitals. No one went the extra mile to administer pain medication, but she was sure they marked it in her chart that they had.

The clock on the wall ticked, and she watched the second hand go around the face. For the past three hours, the woman with the luminous long blonde hair had sat on the edge of the bed, her face still turned away. Occasionally the woman repeated: "Every action has an equal and opposite reaction."

Bailey pleaded her apology. After an hour and a half of apologizing and not receiving a response, she gave up and accepted that the woman was her additional weight to carry. Her equal and opposite reaction for driving drunk and taking this woman's life.

As the sun rose and its rays slipped through the window blinds in her room, Bailey's eyes became heavy and she allowed herself to sleep.

"Every action has an equal and opposite reaction."

Her eyelids flapped open, and she looked at the woman. She had not moved but spoke that same sentence again. Bailey silently dismissed the woman and drifted off to sleep again.

"Every action has an equal and opposite reaction."

She opened her eyes. The woman still sat in the same spot she had been most of the night. Every time she tried to sleep, the woman spoke that sentence repeatedly until Bailey woke up.

She'd gone the whole night without a wink of sleep.

———

The day was a blur for Bailey. Nurses came and went. Hargrave entered the room with a sinister smile to check on his "special case." Physical therapists talked to her about therapy appointments. Her lawyer made an appearance, accompanied by a police officer. The officer was now stationed 24/7 outside her room until she was well enough to be discharged to a minimum-security prison, where she'd stay until her court date—a date stalled by her recovery. The woman sat at the edge of the bed the whole time through all the bustle of people coming and going. During the moments when it was only her and the woman, Bailey would try to sleep, only to be woken.

"Every action has an equal and opposite reaction."

"Will you please stop that!"

The woman made no response or movement. Bailey pushed her bed tray forward, trying to hit the woman to get a reaction. The tray rolled right through her.

"You are either a ghost or a figment of my imagination," Bailey said. "And I think you're the latter because you stayed the entire time people were in and out."

She reached for the remote and turned on the television, aimlessly switching through the channels until she found *Jeopardy!* and settled on the soothing sound of Alex Trebek's voice. Once more, she felt herself growing drowsy and began to slip off to sleep.

"Every action has an equal and opposite reaction."

"Fuck you!" Bailey screamed and threw the remote at the woman. It sailed through her form and smashed against the wall, breaking apart and spilling the batteries onto the linoleum floor.

———

Bailey had been awake and in excruciating pain for nearly forty-eight hours. She had been unable to catch as much as a catnap without being awakened by that damned woman. Her lawyer had been by, yet again, accompanied by an officer—a different one this time; but she didn't remember what they looked like. Her lawyer tried to get her to take a plea deal . . . or maybe plead insanity and talk of an abusive family home life coupled with the demoralizing life as a model who couldn't hack it. She couldn't remember. The only thing she could remember was confessing her guilt over and over again. She swore that the woman's hair glowed brighter with every admission. At one point, her lawyer dismissed Bailey and left. Hargrave never appeared that day, or at least she didn't think so. Time blurred into a nonlinear, amorphous mass.

Exhaustion and pain badgered her body, yet she continued to remain silent against asking for help. No drugs. She must feel the pain. Experience the results of her actions. Yet, at the same time, she wished the agony was over. She wanted the memories . . . the pain . . . gone.

Bailey spoke to the woman, her voice grating like gravel. "I wish I could trade places with you."

The woman's hair darkened to a dull blonde.

"I wish I was the one who was dead and you were still alive," Bailey said.

The woman did not move or speak. Bailey's head lolled on her pillow. She was so tired, so fucking tired.

"Every action has an equal and opposite reaction," said the woman.

Bailey widened her eyes and inhaled sharply. "Stop! I said I was sorry."

Next to the wall under the window, the bed tray rolled over to her and settled over Bailey's lap as if she were about to eat a meal. Pain shot up her leg as the head of the bed raised her to a partially sitting position. The remote was in her hand for the bed's adjustments, but Bailey didn't remember hitting the button or even picking up the remote.

She placed a hand on the top of the tray and breathed into the pain. Feeling the lip of the bed tray, her thumb bumped a button. The top of the tray hinged up, pushing away her hand to reveal a mirror. Familiar eyes and a shattered face reflected at her. A line, starting at the side of her nose, traced the form of a crescent cut up toward the corner of her right eye. Black threaded stitches, akin to spider legs, held the incision closed. Underneath the skin, which she was sure wasn't grafted from her own body, lay the hard metal infused with what she believed to be a smashed truck bumper and dead woman's bones.

These parts—they weren't hers. Hargrave had taken the wreckage of her sin and turned her into a monster. She needed these parts out of her body. With the bed remote in her hand, she smashed the device into the mirror, shattering it into pieces that no longer reflected who she once was.

Bailey plucked a shard out of the frame the length of her hand with a base wide enough to grasp. In the pieces of mirror still set in the frame, she set her eyes on what she had become. With the point of the shard, she pushed the sharp tip into the stitch closest to her nose. One by one, she cut open every stitch with a slow and decisive motion, savoring the snapping sound of the thread.

Once all the sutures were cut, she looked at the woman, still in her same place and silent. Bailey pushed a finger into the incision and peeled apart the flesh that had started to heal. Using the mirror shard, she teased the newly formed connective tissue away, exposing the gleaming metal underneath.

Bailey touched the metal. It was as warm as the blood flowing down her face and chest onto the crisp white hospital sheets. With a deep breath, she slipped her finger to the top ridge of the metal. The pain: excruciating. She accepted each painful moment without crying out as it electrified her body.

"This isn't me." She jammed her finger behind the metal that fused her shattered orbital bones. With a strength she had not felt since before the accident, she yanked until the screws snapped loose and the metal detached from her bones.

The vision in her right eye changed as the orb was now held in place only by muscle. She pushed away the bed tray and unraveled the gauze around her leg. The sight of the two-toned skin took her breath away, and she fingered the grafted skin that wasn't her own. She set the mirror shard to follow the route already mapped in her sutured skin, starting near her hip and leading to her knee.

"Every action has an equal and opposite reaction," the woman said as the mirror shard cut through the first stitch on Bailey's thigh.

In The Hollow of Smugglers' Notch

Snot dripped from Andrew's nose and over his lips. He clamped his mouth tight against the mucus because he couldn't wipe it away—not with a climbing rope clenched tightly between his hands. Andrew leaned over the cliff's edge and looked through his amber-tinted goggles at Terry, who was secured by a single ice axe and the rope. A damning sound echoed across the chilled Vermont air. The reverberation popped as if metal cables were being stretched to their limit. The ice began to crack. Andrew clamped down on the rope, holding the brake harder through his belay device. His forearms shook and ached from holding the rope taut. Tighter than needed, but he didn't want to give the rope an inch.

Terry's grip started to slip down his axe handle. The ice against which he'd planted his crampons gave way when he attempted to set his second axe. Andrew wished they were drinking beer by the firepit in Terry's backyard. But no. They were a couple hundred feet high, climbing Smugglers' Notch on a pitch called Ragnarök. It felt like the end of the world as he hung onto the lifeline that suspended Terry.

Over the past several years, Andrew and Terry had traveled the world to ice-climb some of the most notorious and treacherous routes—never once experiencing a serious accident.

Andrew tried wiping the snot off his lips with his shoulder before shouting encouragements to Terry. "Only a little farther; get that second axe set and pull yourself up. You got this!"

Terry hung just below Andrew's feet. Andrew was torn between maintaining his hold on the rope or releasing it and reaching for Terry.

Terry gritted his teeth as he looked up at Andrew. "If I set the other axe, this ice will give. It's too thin."

Terry's second axe dangled from his wrist at his side. Sharp, sparkling cracks spiderwebbed beneath the surface of the ice cresting the cliff. They should have paid better attention to the weather. It had become unseasonably warm in Vermont over the past few days—an amateur mistake.

Andrew tried to remain calm and thought of another rescue option—an option that risked both of them plummeting over the edge. "It's all good, man. Just let go. I'll try to pull you up."

"What's your anchor?"

Attached to his harness by a length of webbing, ten feet behind Andrew, were two backup anchors screwed into the ice. The main anchor point had failed, uprooting from the fragile ice. He had always used this three-point setup without an issue.

Andrew yelped as he was wrenched forward. Terry dangled midair from his harness, arms and legs flailing. The patch of ice under his only set axe gave way and detached from the mountain, falling into the valley below. Terry's weight pulled a backup anchor out of the ice, and Andrew nearly went over the edge. He fell to his back by instinct, caught traction on a rocky patch of ground, and avoided being dragged over.

Terry hung suspended by Andrew's sheer strength and the last anchor point. If that last point let loose, both men would fall onto the jagged rocks below.

"It's okay," Terry's voice trembled. "Just let go. No sense in both of us dying."

"No!" Andrew shouted. "I'm not losing you."

Terry made no reply. Andrew knew Terry would do the same for him if the roles were reversed. They had the kind of best-friend relationship that most people were envious of and could never find for themselves. Andrew would go as far as to say they were brothers, just not by blood.

"Think about Sheena," Andrew said, trying to encourage Terry. A small agonizing sob sounded from below the edge of the pitch, and Andrew knew that comment hit hard.

Andrew hefted Terry's weight with his left hand, then pulled the slack of the rope through the belay device and braked with his right: Pull up Terry, pull out the slack, and brake; pull up Terry, pull out the slack, and brake. Relief swept over Andrew as Terry's lime-colored glove reached for the cliff's edge and took hold. Breaking all protocol, Andrew dropped the rope and reached for his friend's hand. Terry grabbed Andrew and swung up his left foot, his sharp crampon contacting against the cliff's rock.

A cracking sound thundered around them. Andrew and Terry made eye contact; a silent "I'm sorry" was shared between them as their world shifted. Andrew's fingers dug into Terry's hand. The ground opened beneath him, and the inside of the mountain showed itself. Never letting go of Terry, Andrew pulled his best friend down into the darkness with him.

The hollowness of the Smugglers' Notch was revealed.

———

Pain welled behind Andrew's eyes as he opened them. A black halo around the edge of his vision formed a cone with a small hole of light at the end. He groaned as he took off his glove and felt his forehead. A wet and sharp stinging sensation came from his right temple. Blood covered his fingertips. Head trauma. He rolled his head back and forth on the ground, trying to clear his vision and the pain. When he reopened his eyes, everything came into focus and he realized that he lay in a dark cave. The hole of light was a hole in the cave's ceiling. He'd fallen into the mountain.

He had no idea how long he lay there. They had started climbing at eight that morning and reached the summit a few hours later. It must be around noon, given the brightness of the sky. The cave ceiling looked to be about twenty feet above. Taking inventory of his body, he found himself only banged up. His thick winter wear must have absorbed the impact. Despite the damage to his head, his body only felt bruised.

Climbing rope lay strewn about and still looped through his carabiner and belay device. He assumed the rope had caught him somehow, slowing his fall, as a plunge from that height would have seriously injured or killed him.

The sound of vomiting reminded Andrew that he wasn't alone. Terry, who sat several feet from him—alive—let loose his breakfast of coffee and a bagel with cream cheese.

"An-drew?" Terry said as he wiped his mouth. His curly black hair was matted flat against the right side of his head. Andrew shuffled over to his friend; a new pain, like a deep bruise, throbbed through his hip.

"Everything hurts," Terry whispered.

"We took a long tumble." Andrew knelt and inspected Terry's head. "I think you cracked your head open."

Panic reflected in Terry's eyes as he reached his gloved hand up to his head. Andrew pushed away his hand. "Don't touch it. It's clotting. You'll break it open."

Strangely, they had injured the same side of their heads—nearly in the same place. Terry's cut seemed worse than his own, but neither injury was severe enough to bleed out.

Terry sighed and looked up toward the hole. Andrew followed suit. The blue sky was turning a misty purple.

Andrew began to rethink the time. The color of the sky signaled twilight. It wasn't noon, after all.

"How?" Terry asked, his voice cracking before his eyes began to roll wildly. Andrew steadied his friend, worried about a seizure, but it was only a second before Terry's face returned to normal.

"No clue."

"At least those lights won't leave us in total darkness when night comes..."

"Lights?" Andrew asked with his eyes closed, but Terry didn't respond. He assumed Terry meant the light from the hole. It didn't matter. What mattered was getting both of them patched up and out of this situation. Andrew always had a medical kit with him but had left it along with their other gear at the base of the climb. The plan had been to ascend to the summit and repel back down in one day. He improvised and removed his jacket, long-sleeved T-shirt, and base layer. He then tore at his base layer, making strips that would be effective bandages for their heads. Working on Terry's head, Andrew got his friend properly bandaged to keep dirt out of the wound. The laceration had already clotted faster than expected, and bleeding was no longer a worry. Once Terry woke, Andrew would have his friend do the same with his head injury. While he wasn't overtly bleeding, he wanted to keep the wound as clean and protected as possible.

After finishing with Terry, he put on his long-sleeve T-shirt and jacket, set to work on untying the Prusik knot on Terry's climbing harness, and collected the rope into a neat coil. He put his belay device in the middle of the coil along with the locking carabiner and a cam that would fit a two-inch crack. Andrew then took off his harness and maneuvered Terry out of his before adding both to the pile. Strangely enough, both sets of crampons attached to their feet were gone, along with the rest of the cams and anchors clipped to their harnesses. The webbing was missing as well. He was about to search for the missing components when Terry mumbled about something needing to go away.

"Stop making that sound?"

Andrew responded, "What sound?"

"The clicking."

"I don't hear clicking."

"It is probably just the ice or the cave settling," Terry said, his voice hoarse.

"Um, okay."

"Do you think this is one of the sinkholes?"

"Your guess is as good as mine."

"It has to be. A hollow mountain, just like the holes."

"Well, if this is a sinkhole, we are doing way better off than that research team in Brazil or those Seven Trumpet nutcases," Andrew muttered.

Sinkholes had opened across the world six months ago. Rio de Janeiro had the most recent and largest sinkhole. An entire city block had slipped into the Earth—buildings, cars, people, everything on that block . . . gone. Witnesses across the city said there was a deep trumpet blast before the buildings sank, then an eerie silence took over the moment the city block disappeared. It was as though the hole had stood there since the dawn of time and the city had been built around it.

Rio had the first crewed trip to descend into a sinkhole. No one knew what caused the holes or how deep they were. The world agreed it was time for a human-crewed research expedition, since the initial drone missions lost signal and disappeared ten minutes into a descent. It's unknown if the six members of the Rio team reached the bottom. Radio transmissions didn't work in the sinkhole, and each line that lowered an explorer experienced a long, hard tug at about five hundred feet down. When the tension was released and the cables hauled back to the surface, all the lines were frayed or torn.

As the research team mourned the loss of their contemporaries and launched into planning other options, the pilgrimage of the Seven Trumpets arrived. A crazed cult, dreamed up by Martin Pinchot, had started in the southwestern United States after the sinkholes began to appear. Pinchot convinced his followers that the holes were a sign from God as portals to the Promised Land. The Brazilian government had poorly secured Rio's sinkhole, and Pinchot led the Seven Trumpets to become the first to die by mass sinkhole suicide. His followers held hands around the hole, sang praises, and thanked the Lord for being spared from eternal damnation. After the final prayer, all 984 members of the Seven Trumpets jumped into the Rio sinkhole, falling in the opposite direction of Heaven.

"I'm sick of people being mindless. Making up reasons why the sinkholes exist without solid evidence," Terry grumbled. "People blindly follow whatever the internet says instead of listening to the experts."

"I'm disappointed that the sinkholes are not being created by dinosaurs trying to escape from the center of the Earth and reclaim the surface world as their own again," Andrew said.

"Thank God that's not true, or we'd be raptor food by now." Then Terry added, "The truth is that aliens are farming the planet's core for rich minerals, and the sinkholes are access ports for spaceships."

Andrew laughed. "Give me a break! Do you see any aliens or spaceships down here?" Their laughter echoed through the cave. Despite their current predicament, Terry could still make Andrew laugh.

"I'm not so sure about that," Terry said, his voice waning. "What's all over the ceiling?"

Andrew looked up and squinted. He could make out smaller lights dotting the cave ceiling around the hole. The light outside the hole continued to fade. "Might be mushrooms. I once read about a bio-luminescent fungus that grew in caves."

"Alien eggs," Terry whispered.

Andrew laughed. "Alright, Mulder; we need to stop screwing around and get out of here."

Terry didn't respond.

"Hey, man," Andrew said, remembering that his head wound was still exposed. "Would you mind wrapping this around my head to cover this cut or whatever it is?" He pulled the strips of his base layer out of his jacket pocket. There was still no reply from Terry.

Andrew looked over at him. Terry was on his back with his eyes closed.

"Terry?" Andrew poked him in the side. Terry was out.

"Great," he mumbled, trying to tie the fabric around his head. He couldn't get it set just right or tight enough. The material kept slipping down over his eyes.

"Augh!" Andrew yelled out in frustration and threw the fabric as far as he could.

He stood and paced, angry at the situation they were currently in. They needed to get out of this cave and find help. This was their last climb before Terry married Sheena—his female version—also an avid backpacker and climber. After the wedding, Terry and his new wife planned to be off on their adventures, moving away from their hometown of Deimos, Pennsylvania—without Andrew. A hollow stretched through his chest, causing his chin to tremble. But he wanted nothing but the best for his friend, even if that meant they would have fewer adventures together in the future.

The emptiness in his chest traveled to his abdomen, where his stomach growled. With no food or water, they were in a pickle. They had eaten and drunk what they had on themselves at the midpoint of the climb during their planned rest. Even if they managed to find water in the cave, they had nothing to carry it in. Their empty water bottles had been left where they had rested; they had planned to collect them on the descent—yet another amateur mistake.

To add to the dismal situation, most of the gear they had had on them was mysteriously gone, aside from the single rope, two harnesses, a cam, and his belay device. The right equipment to repel with, but not enough to support climbing out of the cave.

Andrew removed his jacket and balled it up behind his head as he laid down beside Terry. The temperature inside the cave was comfortable. Caves tended to maintain the same temperature year-round despite the outdoor weather conditions, but he was sure it was warmer than average cave temperatures.

He heard the faint clicking Terry had mentioned earlier. It was soft but sharp and emanated from the dark corner of the cave off to his right. The clicking stayed steady and, combined with the lulling sound of Terry's breathing, caused Andrew's eyelids to grow heavy.

"No!" he yelled and sat up. Now wasn't the time to sleep. Andrew climbed to his feet. His head throbbed as he stood, wincing in pain as it felt like his brain was being squished in a vice. Dehydration. He needed to try to find water, even if that meant putting his face right into a dirty puddle. But given the cave's darkness, he didn't know how to see it. The bioluminescent fungus, or whatever was on the ceiling, didn't provide enough light. He didn't have a flashlight, as Terry shunned carrying items like that.

"It weighs me down," Terry always said. Andrew told him to act like a Boy Scout—be prepared. He now regretted the remark because here he was without a flashlight.

Andrew walked over to the wall next to a ledge about eight feet high and the length of a small sedan. He jumped, and his fingers grasped onto the edge. Kicking his feet against the wall, he half-pulled, half-walked himself up in order to peer over. A solid wall stood stark against the back side of the ledge, no way out. He dropped back to the floor of the cave. From his observation, the cave wall was smooth up to the stalactites. He ran his hand over the wall surface in front of him. No, that wasn't true. The walls were covered in striations. He leaned his face in closer. The texture had a pattern, and it ran vertically, not horizontally. Scanning other areas of the wall, he saw that the pattern was the same. The striations, he assumed, went the whole way up.

"Shit." He stepped back. The markings looked like scratches. Holding a hand to the wall, he walked and felt the texture repeat itself. The pitch of Smugglers' Notch caving in on itself didn't seem natural. Something had hollowed out the mountain. Andrew's stomach soured.

"What are you doing?" Terry woke and half leaned up on his side.

"I am looking for a way out. I think . . . I think something dug out the inside of this mountain." Andrew held his hand back up to the wall and started walking toward the darkest part of the cave.

Terry coughed. "Where's all the dirt?"

"Huh?" Andrew stopped.

"The dirt. Where'd all the dirt go if something hollowed out this mountain?"

Andrew hadn't thought about that. Terry was right. There were no dirt piles around. And where was all the debris from the rock from the top of the mountain that fell in with them? Within the lit area of the cave, he could see only Terry and the length of the coiled rope. No rocks, no dirt, no ice. He picked at the rock wall—another oddity to add to the list, along with their missing gear.

"Are you okay?" Terry asked.

"Yep. Following the cave wall into that dark part." He pointed to the area shrouded by the bioluminescent light.

Terry got up and walked over to him.

"Look," Andrew said, running a hand on the wall.

Terry shrugged and echoed Andrew's initially dismissed thoughts. "Erosion, probably."

"From what?"

"Maybe there was water in here at one point. I don't know. Does it matter?"

"All the lines are perfectly vertical. Water is fluid; there would be different patterns throughout. It matters because maybe something dug this hole out. And it might be in here with us. The clicking sound."

"Is likely water dripping somewhere off deeper in the cave. Do you really think something's in here with us? Come on, man. We'd know by now." Terry laughed. "Are you taking those stories about the sinkholes seriously?"

Andrew chewed at the inside of his cheeks. A chill went through him as he thought there was more to their surroundings than being trapped inside a water-eroded mountain. Running a hand along the wall, he walked into the dark part of the cave and found a small tunnel. The clicking emanated from inside. It never changed cadence, so whatever was making it had to be inanimate. Terry was right; nothing could click that long at the same tempo and be alive.

This tunnel could be a way out. A sweat broke out on Andrews's forehead as he entered the pitch-black tunnel. How far did this reach into the mountain? What if it only took them deeper inside? What if there was no way out except for how they had come in?

He took a few more steps forward into the tunnel and abruptly stopped. Something felt wrong. Terry bumped into the back of him, and Andrew felt his stomach drop to his feet. He almost fell forward, forward into the darkness. He had no idea what was before him, but the clicking was louder. A wind tickled the underside of his jaw, coming up from the ground.

"Stop," he whispered. Terry complied.

"Well, that sound is definitely coming from this tunnel. It has to be water dripping on metal or something similar to make that clicking sound. There's got to be something man-made in here, right?" Terry started.

Andrew frowned. The sound emanated from below him. Keeping one hand against the wall, Andrew bent down and blindly reached with his other hand to feel the wind. His hand continued down to the point where he stretched below the level of his feet. Wind passed through his fingers.

"Don't move."

"What are you doing?" Terry asked.

"Fuck!"

"What?"

"Hold on." Andrew sat and lowered his left leg into the opening before him. The pain burned up his hip, but he needed to get a sense of the depth. His foot connected with nothing but air.

"There's a big hole right here," he said.

"Really? Can you see it?" Terry asked. "It's so dark, I can't even see you." Andrew yelped and slipped forward. Terry had stepped on his hand. He pushed Terry backward violently as he pulled his leg up and crawled away from the hole.

"Dammit! You nearly pushed me in!" Andrew shook his injured hand and looked at the silhouette of his friend backing away.

"Sorry man . . .," Terry mumbled as he walked out of the tunnel and into the lit section of the cave.

"It's okay." Andrew's chin quivered as he crouched next to the hole. He felt bad for snapping at Terry. He'd always been known to have a level head in stressful situations, but this situation had pushed Andrew well beyond his limits.

The hole stood about ten feet inside the tunnel. Andrew slid his hands along the edge, trying to see if any ground went around the hole they could walk on. Nothing. From what he could feel, the hole took up the entire interior of the tunnel's floor. There was no way around it.

Andrew sat back on his heels. The only way out of this mountain was down this hole or up the way they had fallen in. They could rappel into the hole, but without being able to see, it could be a suicide descent. He didn't know how deep it went, and there was no guarantee that an exit was even down there. Andrew stood and walked out of the tunnel. He huffed as he sat beside his friend, who was lying on his back and looking at the ceiling.

"Ever see anything like that before?" Terry asked. "It's like stuff is moving in the lights."

Andrew looked up but didn't see anything moving. Ignoring Terry, he said, "We will have to rappel out of here. Down that hole."

"Why?"

"It's the only way out because we are not climbing those straight walls without axes and crampons. We have only one cam to use as an anchor." Andrew held up his hand. "Before you say it, I know it's risky."

"Then let's just wait for someone to find us."

"We aren't due home for three more days, and Sheena is used to you not calling her when we are out climbing."

"That's not what I meant. When did you activate the PLB?" Terry sat up and asked.

"Your WHAT?" Andrew shouted, and the clicking from the hole stopped. He looked toward the tunnel.

"My personal locater beacon. It signals for—"

"I know what a PLB is," Andrew snapped at Terry. He shoved aside the thoughts about the clicking as, this time, he didn't feel guilty about yelling at his friend. "You've had one this whole time? Why didn't YOU activate it?"

"Because I wasn't all that coherent earlier . . . and thought I gave it to you," Terry said, patting his left chest pocket. A thin frown formed on his face, acknowledging that he had not given the PLB to Andrew.

"What the fuck! We could have been rescued already!"

Terry unzipped the pocket and removed a small device slightly longer than his hand. He pulled off a glove and gave Andrew a confused look.

"It is warm in here."

"Does it matter? Just activate that damn thing, and let's get out of here."

Terry fiddled with the device. "What's your problem, man?"

Andrew sighed. "I've been wracking my brain on how to save us. And you had the answer in your pocket this whole time."

Tears shimmered in Terry's eyes, but he said nothing. He clicked a button, activating a bright strobe light that flashed with a sharp staccato.

"Can't you turn the strobe off and make it a solid light?" Andrew asked, shielding his face from the flash. His eyes had grown so accustomed to the cave's dim light that the strobe was causing him to see nothing but white. Plus, he would prefer to conserve the battery and use the light as a flashlight if a rescue party couldn't find them. The light was bright enough to illuminate the entirety of the cave with each flash—even revealing the tunnel.

"It's the emergency strobe so that someone can see us," Terry replied as he too shielded his eyes.

"So we can't use it like a flashlight?"

"No. And leaving it right here is best. It sends out a digital signal to a rescue satellite system. I'd rather keep it where it has the best line of sight to the sky." Terry pointed up toward the hole in the cave's ceiling.

Andrew couldn't handle the light. The pulsations made his head throb, and Terry seemed to feel the same way by the way he had his hand up to the dressed head wound. Andrew stood and walked toward the small ledge in the wall on the other side of the cave, wanting to get as far away from the light as possible.

He turned to say something to Terry, but movement at the tunnel shifted in the bright flash of the strobe, causing him to stop. Andrew rubbed his eyes; the light had to be playing tricks on his vision.

"Let's put some distance between us and the strobe." Andrew pointed to the ledge. Terry seemed to float as he walked toward Andrew in the wake of the strobe's flashes. A tingle of electricity shot up Andrew's spine. Behind Terry, something actually moved. A large, bulbous form skittered from the tunnel, scratching across the floor and clicking as it came toward them. The flash of the strobe light made the creature look as if it was moving in slow motion.

"Terry!" Andrew pointed over Terry's shoulder. "Run!"

"What?"

"Something's coming."

"There's nothing—"

"Run!" Andrew screamed and turned toward the ledge. Footsteps behind him marked that Terry was following, but not very fast.

"I don't see any—"

A loud crunch stilled Andrew's heart. The flashing stopped. The only light source in the cave came from the glowing stalactites, which had dimmed since the strobe started.

"Hurry!" Andrew urged as they reached the ledge. He jumped and caught the edge; walking his feet against the wall, he pulled himself up and over onto the ledge. Andrew rolled to his stomach and, anchoring his left hand on the edge, reached for Terry with his right, as his friend—at five-foot-five—was too short to get up by himself. Terry had picked up speed and was within arm's reach.

The stalactite lights continued to dim, darkening the interior of the cave. Andrew could barely make out Terry's outstretched lime glove and face. Andrew reached for his friend, their fingertips inches apart. His heart pounded, shooting pain down his arm. Whatever had crawled out of the tunnel closed in on them.

Terry's face went slack. "Help."

Andrew toed the ground, sliding forward to gain a few more precious inches. His fingers tapped Terry's fingertips. The contact urged him to slide further, but his shoulder and head dipped as his legs lifted from the ground. His balance faltered, threatening to topple him to the cave's floor. Andrew wiggled his hips to scooch himself back—losing those gained inches. He couldn't reach Terry, and Andrew stared at the lime glove as Terry's pleas to be saved echoed in his ears.

The glove disappeared in the darkness as a scream ripped through the interior of the hollow mountain, drowning out the sounds of the creature's clicking.

"No," Andrew moaned.

Terry's scream cut off abruptly. Tearing and slurping and chewing reverberated off the cave walls. Andrew slid away from the ledge, away from the creature, away from his best friend. He curled himself into a ball against the rock wall, trying to make himself invisible as he cried to the crunching sounds of Terry being eaten.

Overhead, the dim light of the stalactites began to pulsate.

———

Survival overtook Andrew's exhaustion. He flailed his arms, trying to hit whatever shook him awake. A warm blue light filled the cave, and he could see the whole interior. In front of him stood someone in a red parka. A rescue team had arrived.

"Terry?" he asked, hoping that what had happened to his friend was only a nightmare.

"No," a feminine voice answered, her face hidden by the parka's hood. "You are the only one here." She touched his head right where he had bashed up his temple. A blazing hot white flash flooded his vision, followed by the feeling of something sharp being shoved into his brain. He let out a ragged breath and slapped her hand away. When his sight returned, he saw that she had her gloved hand up under the hood.

"What the fuck!" he yelled at her.

"We are here for you," she said.

Andrew sat up and looked past her, searching for Terry. The PLB had done its job, and a rescue party had found them. He saw two more rescuers wearing similar red parkas, but no Terry. And there was no sign of whatever had taken him. The other rescuers were by the tunnel, and he could see the edge of the hole inside the tunnel in the brighter cave light. One of the rescuers knelt and picked something up off the ground next to the hole. Andrew pushed past the woman, slid off the ledge, and hobbled over to them. Andrew shielded his eyes with a hand. The stalactites shone brilliantly. Too brightly. Within them, something undulated like a pupa before it split open and a butterfly was born.

"Get away! There's something in there," Andrew yelled, waving his arms above his head as he limped toward the other rescuers. Neither said anything, but the one kneeling next to the hole held out something to Andrew.

A bloodied lime glove.

He gasped and took a step back. The clicking sound started again from the hole. *It was coming.* Andrew backed away and bumped up against something hard.

It was the woman.

"It's coming! We have to get outta here. Now!" He grabbed her arm and tried to pull her away.

She stood like a boulder, her tiny frame holding fast against Andrew's strength.

"Will you stay to serve our Lords?" she asked.

"Lady, What? What . . . ? No, just no. We have to leave." Andrew looked about the cave. No ropes hung from the hole in the ceiling. And he saw no machinery or apparatus that would lift them out.

"We, the children of the demiurge, born of Duraik and Igros, have been brought here to repurpose this planet." She kept her head bowed as she spoke. "You do not wish to join us as a servant to our Lords?"

He grasped the uninjured side of his head and looked wildly at her. "What? Demiurge? Derek and Icarus . . . ? What the hell are you talking about?" He let go of his head and shook his hands at her. "You know what, it doesn't matter. We have to go!"

"There is nowhere for you to go, child of Ja. You have chosen your fate."

"Child of *who*?" he asked.

She lifted her head slightly, and Andrew saw her mouth underneath the parka's hood. Her lips were closed and smeared with the blood from his head. He stepped back, but her hand shot out and grabbed him by the arm.

Andrew tried to pull away, but she held fast. Something throbbed behind her lips and cheeks as if trying to push through her flesh. Her lips parted as two thick, barb-covered black pincers emerged. Yellowish ooze trickled from lacerations to her skin caused by the barbs. The pincers clicked together, displaying their muscular power.

Andrew tried to push her away but to no avail. She raised her chin, pincers jutting toward him. The parka's hood slipped from her head, revealing her entire face. Her eyes were coal black and shiny, like a beetle's.

Achromatopsia

Nearly five years ago my life fell to pieces and I died—then came back to life, much to everyone's surprise (or chagrin). In the end, everyone believed me to be weak. And they weren't entirely wrong. A long-term relationship crumbled under the weight of gaslighting, manipulation, and narcissism. At first my family and friends marveled at my strength in initiating the split, leaving behind a newly purchased home (which I paid more than half the down payment out of pocket) and a well-off, stable life during a global pandemic.

I wasn't strong. I jumped out of that relationship without a plan and focused on the belief that had I stayed with my ex, the weight of his abuse would have crushed me. Despite the best intentions of escaping for my mental health, I'd fallen along with the disintegrating economy and declining global health. I lost my high-paying job a few months after using all my retirement funds to move into a two-thousand-dollars-a-month condo. I would be evicted before making it six months into my new life. The loss of my savings and home lured me to the railing of my condo's third-floor balcony, where I jumped . . . for real.

But just like all my other failures in life, I failed to kill myself.

Broken bones, a sliced liver, and head trauma followed me into a year-and-a-half-long rehabilitation. Scars, pins, surgeries, therapy, and a mountain of medical debt now haunted me. My vision is jacked up where the world has lost all its color, and I have weird phantom sensations all over my body that I can't pinpoint. It's like I am being touched but am not. The neurosurgeon says it's from my traumatic brain injury.

"You have a demon who rode your back out of hell." Amelia's eyes were emotionless and cold as she looked at me as I lay in a hospital bed after what we believed was my last surgery. Mom made her come to the hospital, and I didn't know if the look in her eyes was from that or from the pain she constantly carried. She and I were both victims of trauma and abuse from men. Almost two years before my biggest personal failure and global pandemic, I was pretty well off and had helped her through her situation with money and moral support. She went through a nasty breakup with her ex, who stole her identity and left her bankrupt. During the summer after the breakup, her two girlfriends thought she needed an escape and took her backpacking.

Something happened to her out there. No one knows for sure what. And no one is talking. Her friends, Ellie and Sheena, said she left their tent to go to the bathroom and returned several hours later ... different. They wouldn't look me in the eyes as they told me the story. I didn't believe them.

When I needed Amelia the most, all she could do was either point out my failure or look silently off in the distance—ignoring everyone around her. This Amelia is vacant and hollow. She's dead inside.

And she looked even more dead to me with my new condition. My ... brain injury. Amelia was a dirty shade of gray, and at times it was hard to differentiate her from the darker gray curtain behind her. My vision was permanently fucked.

"We're cursed, Sis," I said, ignoring her demon comment because she's messed up too.

"Maybe it's this town . . .," she mused. There was a slight twitch to the corner of her lip—a sly smile. I stared hard at her face while she vacantly looked out the window. The pregnant silence that separated us was in spirit only as I listened to the monitors attached to me mark out the rhythm of my beating heart. She's right. And I needed to get out of this town.

We needed to get out of this haunted town of Deimos. It was full of too many of our ghosts.

———

Our mother died shortly after my final surgery. She left us a large inheritance. We used it all to pay off our debts, but now we're left with nothing except our mother's house. Or so we thought.

"The house . . .." I sat across the kitchen table from Amelia. The paper in my hands, a letter from Mom's mortgage lender, crinkled in my nervous hands. Amelia had her usual blank look and sat straight in the chair, hands folded in her lap. She looked like a mannequin. The house would be foreclosed since neither of us could afford the mortgage. Our childhood home. The one our father died building. Mom took out a second mortgage to hire contractors to finish the work. I began to sweat. Could the bank go after the money she had left to us? The money I had already spent. Worry tore at my insides as I felt I was about to be consumed by debt again.

"So," Amelia said.

"Don't you care? We're going to lose our home."

"I don't care."

I stood, slamming the letter down on top of the clothed table. Mom had covered the table with an orange and black plaid table-cloth before she passed away from a massive heart attack in the upstairs hallway. She was getting the Halloween decorations out of the attic. I found her at the base of the ladder, her body covered with the contents of the box she'd carried: rubbery black bats, gossamer spiderwebs, and little multicolored plastic skulls. Decorations she'd hang from the branches of the tall, opulent Japanese red maple out in the front yard. An ache in my chest throbbed at the thought of never again seeing the beautiful tree's colors, with Mother hanging the decorations in the branches.

Amelia immediately disappeared into her bedroom when she came up the stairs after hearing me scream at the sight of our mother's broken form lying on the floor with her eyes unblinking toward the ceiling. My sister closed the door on me and our dead mother. She did this every time she didn't want to deal with something. After the backpacking trip, she'd lost her apartment and moved in with Mom. She'd hide all day and night in her room, coming out only to eat. I would try to coax her from her room by saying positive things about her and life, but she'd never open the door or reply. The only sounds heard from the other side of the door were her whispers: "I am Amelia. I am Amelia. I am Amelia."

This woman in the house . . . I didn't feel like she was my sister anymore. Once, she'd been my protector. She'd saved me countless times from bullies during our middle school years. Amelia towered over everyone at eleven. She swore that she'd always take care of me. Yet she'd abandoned me in my time of need.

Over time, Amelia began to stay out of her room for longer periods. But she still wasn't right in the head. She walked around the house ambivalent about everything. And this Amelia didn't care about our mother's death. She didn't care that we were broke. She didn't care that we were about to be homeless. And she didn't care when I suggested we pack whatever we could into the car and move to Pittsburgh with the thousand dollars I had found hidden in a book on Mom's bookshelf while looking for things to sell.

"What's Pittsburgh?"

I gave Amelia a perplexed look and shook my head. We'd visited the city at least once a year as kids because our cousin lived there. For Christ's sake, it's the second-biggest city in our state. "What the hell is wrong with you?"

She shrugged her shoulder; the cold, vacant look in her eyes never wavered.

She was my sister, but I began to hate her. Maybe she'd wake up with a new town, a new start. Be herself again. We could only go up from here.

———

"It's shit that you can't see how mismatched your clothes are." Amelia's eyes gave me a once-over. "You do know you have a lime green bra on with bright red shorts? It's fucking March, not Christmas. And those blue heels are ridiculous."

I looked down at my barely-clad body. My skin and clothing were different shades of gray.

"It would help if you'd give me a hand in organizing my clothes by color like I asked."

"And why would I do that? You looking like an exploded clown with your caked makeup and color combos scares your customers my way."

Amelia held an unlit Virginia Slim between her non-nicotine-stained fingers. She thought the skinny cigarettes made her look sexy, but she looked like a five-year-old sucking down a Pixy Stix. She doesn't smoke but once said that just holding the cigarette in her mouth and between her fingers calmed her. I thought it to be more of an oral fixation.

It was our break time, and we sat next to each other in the front pew of St. Paul's Cathedral, staring at the grand stained-glass windows behind the pulpit. I needed a cigarette but was out and had no more money. I thought about asking her for one, but a small sore in the corner of Amelia's lip churned my stomach. I wasn't sure which cigarette in her pack she hadn't already held between her lips, as she tended to put the used ones back in once the filters became too wet from her saliva.

"Sucks that God won't let you see these beautiful windows, Erin. About the only pretty things in this dump except me."

Her vanity was unbecoming. A new attitude I disliked. She had come into her own in this city. I don't know what changed my sister, but living in this rundown old church-turned-bordello had sparked something in her. It's gross. She thrived here.

Amelia pointed to the large stained-glass window directly above us. Immortalized in the window is St. Scholastica, whoever she was. The saint's hand is outstretched, palm up, beckoning us to climb into the window with her.

"I can see the image, just not the colors," I said.

"Shame."

"It's not a shame. It just is what it is." I hated this new version of her. If I couldn't have my original sister back, I would prefer to have the vacant, hollow version we seem to have left in Deimos.

"You are a piece of work. I'd die if I couldn't see all the pretty colors of the world."

"I have to get back to work." A lie. There wasn't anyone waiting for me today.

"Sure. You should probably change your clothes. Your johns will ask for me if they take one look at you."

I didn't respond, then stood and walked away from her. On my way out of the sanctuary, I grabbed a discarded coat off the back pew. Throwing it over my bare shoulders, I patted the pockets. Empty. Some john must have forgotten it as he sat out here waiting for an available girl. This afternoon, six of them sat waiting in the other pews. They'd all asked for other girls today, two specifically for Amelia. And that's fine. While I needed the money, I was too tired. An escape from this hell is what I needed.

This house of God in North Oakland had become an abandoned shell of its former piety when the economy crashed. Now it's a sanctuary for ladies of the night, or that's what Ma'dam said. It's been our home since we arrived in Pittsburgh five years ago. Back then, it was a sanctuary for the homeless. Then Ma'dam took over. We were lucky she kept us around. She instantly loved Amelia—who became her best girl. She said I had a pretty face but was too stout. However, all the extra weight I gained from lying in hospital beds melted off in time. Food was provided to us, though it was mostly bread, soups, and coffee—nothing there to add fat. A stipend was taken from our pay for the food and rent of a little box that served as a bedroom, which can only fit a stained twin bed and a trunk for personal belongings. While each room is private, we share it with our johns when they come knocking.

I made my way to the west bell tower of the cathedral, which had long been condemned and blocked off. But I'd found a way into the tower shortly after we had arrived. It had been my secret hiding place ever since. The bells haven't sounded in years, so no one would need to go up there.

A cool early spring breeze flowed through the bell tower's opening. It was quiet. Once a bustling city, Pittsburgh now existed ominously silent aside from the sporadic passing car. Most couldn't afford gas nowadays. Driving was a luxury.

I leaned on the decaying wood frame that exposed the bell tower to the skies of the metropolitan area once known as the Steel City. Thanks to my cerebral achromatopsia, the city is an old black, white, and gray photograph from the 1920s. Since becoming fully color blind, I barely remember what colors looked like.

"Hiding up here as usual?"

I jumped, but I really shouldn't. He's always around.

"I'm not hiding," I lied, "just thinking."

"About?" Anam, my ever-lurking shadow, asked.

"About how much my life sucks."

"You could leave Amelia and go back to Deimos. Live with your auntie."

"My aunt hasn't spoken to me since I attempted to kill myself. I'm a disgrace."

"And you believe your auntie thinks that?"

"Yes." My fingernails cut into the soft, decaying wood. "It was the last thing she said to me. When I try to contact her, she ignores me. She didn't even come to Mom's funeral because I was there."

He laughed. "Guess it's just you and your sis."

"It is . . ." I continued leaning on the windowsill, staring at the desolate surroundings that used to be full of life.

"You said it yourself; you and she are cursed. Though she's a lot worse off than you are." He laughed again.

"She's worse off than me? How can you say that? At least she's not colorblind."

"Oh, you have no idea. That woman downstairs is a terrible thing. We'd do well to be rid of her."

I lowered my eyes and stared at the sidewalk on the ground outside the bell tower window, resisting the urge to turn and look for him because if I did, he'd disappear. "What the fuck do you mean?"

He ignored my question. "Well, I don't think you're a disgrace. I think you're quite fabulous."

I let his comment about Amelia go. He always said gibberish about her to get a rise out of me. "You're only saying I'm not a disgrace because I got you out of that hell hole. You owe me, you know?"

The bell tower had become stiflingly hot, and I leaned further out the window to breathe in the cool, fresh air.

"I do believe it's the other way around. I broke laws to save you from being sent to Hell and got you out of line in Purgatory after your little fall—even though my job is to recruit souls," Anam said.

"I don't know why." Feelings from that day on my condo balcony, when I stared over the railing at the sidewalk before I jumped, bubbled in my chest, coaxing me to lean further out the bell tower window—words of "what if" swirled about my mind.

The oppressive heat in the room died. I exhaled and fell backward from the window frame onto my butt.

"Careful there," he chuckled; "there is something very special that I need you to do before jumping off another building. Well, two things."

I shook my head to clear the awful feelings and breathed deeply. My throat cracked as I asked, "What? That's not how repayment works. One-for-one deal."

"What I did for you was so large that it counts for two." His voice sounded smug.

"Fine. What do you want?" I looked at the white clouds in a gray sky through the window.

Silence.

"Why are you telling me this now? It's been over five long years of exhausting banter with you, only to be told *now* that you've been expecting repayment." I gritted my teeth. "And here I thought you were just haunting me for shits and giggles."

He laughed. "The time has to be just right before I ask for my first favor."

"Soon?"

"Oh, Cupcake." There was a loud creak behind me as the door to the bell tower opened and quickly closed. I turned to look. Muffled from the other side of the door, I heard him say, "Time's coming soon."

——

The streets during the day were no safer than at night. I kept my walks contained between the cathedral and the little convenience store a block away on Bayard Street. Wandering trips around the city ended last year when one of our girls disappeared when she went to see her mother on Centre Avenue. No one knew what happened to her. More women were abducted to be sold to perverts or into sex rings these days than were raped and murdered. We women have become currency.

I carried my father's old bowie knife on me when I went to the convenience store. When I'm not out, it hides in my bed, the handle barely covered by the mattress.

"I don't know why you carry that thing. I'll keep you safe."

I snorted and continued walking with my head low, but my eyes were alert as I scanned the street ahead and the crumbling buildings on either side. I didn't know which ones were empty or sheltering someone nefarious.

"You'd only selfishly keep me safe. You need me," I muttered, now knowing he had plans for me.

"I do, Cupcake. I do need you."

Anam skulked in the shadows off to my left, staying well out of range of the streetlights and my sight.

"I doubt you'll be lucky tonight. You're better off returning and getting a smoke off Amelia. Grab one from the pack. One she didn't have her diseased lips all over."

I swallow hard as a lump of nausea lodged in my throat at the thought of the sore on the corner of my sister's lip. It became pussier by the day.

"The color's a whiteish green, you know. And there're little red lines around it." He took joy in describing the color of Amelia's cold sore to me.

"Stop. Just stop." While I don't want to think about what was growing on my sister's face, I'm concerned that she's sick. Afraid that she might have caught something off one of her customers.

"Aw, there is a little love left in you for her. Despite how you've grown to despise her over the years, you still have those sisterly feelings deep down."

"Stop reading my mind."

"Not reading your mind. Just your body and facial expressions. No matter how much you try to say you hate that *thing*, you love her—even if she's no longer your sister."

"Enough. That's my sister. She's different because she's damaged like me."

"If that makes you feel better about her change in attitude, well, you do you."

I ignored him and kept walking toward the store, hoping there was a guy outside I could flirt with or pay a favor to get a pack of smokes. I had no money and wasn't lucky like Amelia, to whom Ma'dam provided cigarettes for free due to being her best girl. Every dime I made went to my rent and food stipend. My pay is nowhere near as good as hers or the other girls'. I don't know why. Maybe I'm too skinny now? Too flat-chested and leggy. Amelia told me that guys like women with a bit of meat on their bones, like her. She's voluptuous and toned—the perfect body. I'm too much of a toothpick these days—no longer the stout girl Ma'dam first met.

"You said this place was pretty once?" he asked, trying to initiate small talk, which he started to do a couple of weeks ago. I think it's because the time for my repayment is coming soon. He's trying to butter me up. In no way was this chatter a reflection of his guilt about the comments about Amelia. I'm quite sure he doesn't have a conscience to experience guilt.

"Yea. We always came here to visit my cousin before she got married. You know her wedding was in St. Paul's?"

"I did not."

"Her wedding was the last time we came to the city. She moved to Florida shortly after. I missed coming here. This city used to be a beautiful place." I sighed, remembering the lush greens of the tree-filled city, the many yellow bridges crisscrossing the three rivers, and the tall mirrored skyscrapers that reflected the blue sky. Now

Pittsburgh had become as haunted as every other city and town across the United States.

"The steel industry started coming back to the states. The city was coming alive again. Old decrepit factories of the '80s and '90s were being rejuvenated and modernized. I'd always wanted to live here. But now, this place is dark. It reminds me of Deimos."

"Those pandemics fucked with you humans. Too many back-to-back for *yinz* to handle."

I stop walking, ignoring the Pittsburgh slang. "Do you know what caused the pandemics?"

"Oh, Cupcake. I know everything."

Risking him disappearing, I turned to the shadows on my left in an unlit alleyway. The other side wasn't visible. The void of darkness beckoned, and I considered stepping into it.

"Tell me," I demanded.

"Some things are best left as surprises." He laughed. "Go get your cancer sticks. I'll see you later." And then he was gone.

As he abandoned me, I patted the knife hidden inside my jacket for reassurance.

———

Amelia was asleep in the same pew when I returned to the main sanctuary. All the johns were gone. It seemed she hadn't returned to work or taken on those two who asked for her. She was stretched out, lying on her back upon the faded, stained upholstery with her angelic pale hair neatly piled beneath her head, like a silk pillow. Above her head lay a half-smoked pack of Virginia Slims. I pulled out three cigarettes without waking her. These didn't look like she'd used them, and I prayed I was right. There hadn't been anyone outside the grocery store for me to sweet-talk into buying a pack. Amelia would accuse me of taking them when she woke, but what did I care? She should keep a better watch on her stuff.

Lighting one, I walked to a pew in the back of the sanctuary to hide from her and lay down. Wrapping the jacket tighter around myself, I quickly inhaled the cigarette before someone could yell at me for smoking inside. Even though St. Paul's Cathedral is now a bordello, it technically is still a holy place. I could be such an asshole. Really, what kind of people smoke in a church?

"Damaged people like me," I said aloud as I exhaled a cloud of smoke toward the high domed ceiling. It's ornate, with thick arches built between the columns. Once painted pearl white for purity, the years haven't been kind to this house of God, with everything now having a gray tinge. Even without my vision condition, I'm sure it looked the same as I saw it. Despite only visiting once before the world fell apart, the nave of St. Paul's captivated me with its ethereal, white-colored vaults traced by greige-colored arches as if the ceiling was somehow a gateway to Heaven. When the sunlight shone through the stained-glass windows, they reflected kaleidoscope colors all over the sanctuary. Maybe those multihued windows still had color blazing through them. Though I doubt it; this city was crumbling. God left us to rot in the world they created. They would never abandon their children if they were indeed the One Who Created All. I hated them.

"Ah. You hate your God that much?" He sat somewhere behind my head. I didn't look in his direction and continued to stare at the colorless ceiling.

"Is there even a God?"

"Devil's real."

"Are they? Because last I checked, I was only in Purgatory, not Hell. Never got the sense there is an actual Hell, despite what you say about the matter. Felt like I was in an endless limbo."

"Hell's real. Your Devil's real. I know both well."

I took another drag off my cigarette.

"Those things are going to kill you, Cupcake," he said.

I laughed. "These are the only things in my life that make me feel good."

"And you had to steal them."

I ignored him. There wasn't any point in arguing. It's my curse that I knew him, and he knew me . . . too well.

"Time's coming due."

A weight behind my head shifted as he returned to the shadows within the cathedral. If he could hide in the darkness here, there was no God—and this place wasn't holy.

———

The slap across my face ripped me from a deep sleep.

"What the fuck?" Slap! "Give them back!" Slap!

Amelia had put two and two together that I had stolen some of her cigarettes. I grabbed her hands as she went to hit me again, pulling her down on top of me and then pushing her to the floor. Untangling myself from the jacket, with my arms still inside, I flicked it behind me like a cape. She screamed while pinned beneath me. Our eyes met, and in hers I saw nothing. There was no emotion of rage in her eyes despite words of hate spewing from her mouth. When the old Amelia got angry, her green eyes sparked with a fire that scared anyone who dared look at her. The old Amelia, who was once my protector by keeping the schoolyard bullies away, was now my attacker.

These eyes on Amelia's face were dull and gray—I'm sure that wasn't because of my condition. Maybe Anam was right. Whoever was pinned beneath me, I hated who she had become. This wasn't my sister. Amelia had sworn always to protect me. And now look at where our lives were.

I kicked her in the head as she tried to right herself. She screamed and heaved her weight into the pew, flipping it and me to the floor. My head cracked off the hard floor. The world went black for a moment, and I feared I'd entirely lost my vision. I hadn't. It came right back, just in time to see Amelia's open palm swinging at my face.

"I didn't steal your pack of cigs! I just took one!" *Three really only equates to one*, I thought while holding my head.

"Give me my pack back! Give it to me! It's mine." She went to take another swing but put too much force into it. I ducked, and she fell forward, flipping face-first over the tipped pew.

Like the pop of a bubble, the pent-up anger I had harbored for many years burst. All the sorrow I had from our broken and cursed lives, the hate toward all the terribleness that was put upon us, flowed out of me. And then those words that *he* had spoken to me in the bell tower. About Amelia being some terrible thing . . . I believed Anam. She had become something awful. Inhuman. This wasn't my sister. This wasn't my Amelia.

My hands found the thing's fallen form and gripped its throat.

"The time is here." Anam was behind me. I pulled one hand away from the thing's neck.

There was no pain as my fist connected with the face that once belonged to my sister. Blood burst from its nose as I withdrew. A brilliance of red splashed across its face and dripped down its chest onto the floor.

Exquisite—the red. I'd forgotten about this color. Memories of blooming roses and shiny autumn apples flooded my brain. I looked at the back of my hand, still cast in a grayish tone, along with everything else around the thing and me save for its blood coating my knuckles in red—so many years of living in a colorless, lackluster world.

A deep breath that crackled my larynx surged in my chest as my head tilted back, looking up at the stained-glass windows rimming the top of the cathedral's walls. Red hard-candied chunks sprinkled the black-lead-lined gray and white glass. I returned my gaze to the thing before me and punched it in the face again. More blood gushed from its nose. I laughed with joy at the crimson brilliance. The thing coughed and tried to climb backward to get to its feet.

But it was too slow.

I tore off the jacket and jumped on top of it once more, grabbing it by the throat. Red coated my hands. Red covered its face. Red painted the gray floor beneath us and the overturned pew beside us. The beautiful color—I could see it!

Its hands outstretched, reaching toward the sky. Fingers writhed as though they were trying to grab something to free themselves from my grasp. It never once tried to grab at me.

A convulsion undulated beneath me, and it dug its fingers into the corners of the lips that were once Amelia's and pulled its mouth wide open. Its jaw cracked apart with a crunching pop. The puss-filled sore on the corner of its mouth burst, spraying off-white goop laced with red streaks on my chest as puss oozed down its chin and neck onto my hand. The corners of its lips tore, gushing rivulets of blood carrying bits of cheek flesh to join the rest of the crimson blood that coated the floor. Heavy black smoke shot from the thing's wide maw. I ducked as the smoke flew past my ear, disregarding it as it went by—my focus honed on the red-streaked face before me.

A sigh escaped its broken mouth, sounding like it said my name using my sister's voice. Memories of her calling out to me as children echoed in my head, and I flinched at the thought.

"Thanks for taking care of that terrible little problem." Anam was behind me again, breathing down my neck. "Now, just one more favor."

I could hear him, but his words barely registered in my mind.

"She's dying. How do you feel?" Anam said.

My sister died a long time ago, I thought.

"Your sister's blood is all over your hands. Does it make you sad that you've hurt her? What about guilty? Does it make you want to kill yourself again?" he asked.

The thing's eyes looked at me before rolling about its head. Vacant, hollow, just as they have been since the day Amelia returned home after that hiking trip with her two friends. A gargling sound rattled from the back of its throat as red mucus and saliva dripped from the torn jaw.

"Oh, I'm sure it does. I'll help you make your death more permanent this time, and then—" The hair on the back of my neck rose to meet the sting of Anam's breath. "Our bind will be broken, and I'll be free in this realm."

He was wrong.

"I owe no one," I said, punctuating each word through gritted teeth.

The warmth of the thing's blood comforted my hands and thoughts— all these years of living in a dull, colorless world of constant obligation to now have release blooming beneath my fingertips. I needed to be free.

Thin red bubbles popped from its nostrils as it struggled to breathe. Eyes drift closed. My fingers cupped the side of its head, lightly lifting it toward my own. Its right eyelid cracked open to reveal a softening pupil.

Do you have my sister's green eyes too? I wondered as I gouged my thumbs into its eye sockets.

The Faunling

The creature's eyes were deep blue pools that reminded Dominik Mendez of his daughter's. He dove into them, drunk on feelings of love and obsession. The power contained within its diminutive form was endless, cosmic, irresistible. Dom had to have the little animal as his own.

The creature—a Faunling, he named it—graced his dreams. It sat on the trunk of an uprooted oak tree next to a pond. In the sky, a full moon drifted in a thick black quilt with stars scattered in an unfamiliar pattern. The Faunling was tiny and deerlike, with shimmering blue, forward-facing eyes. If it weren't for a dainty pointed muzzle that ended in a pert suede nose, its face would be eerily similar to a human's.

Two long, fleshy appendages grew from pert ears atop its head. They traveled behind its head only to peek back out over the shoulders of its front legs, as if it wore pigtails. A thin catlike tail waved seductively behind it. The shimmering, iridescent fur of the Faunling reminded him of freshly fallen snow.

Dom needed the Faunling. He had to hold it. However, every step Dom tried to take beyond where he stood caused the ground to stretch far out before him as if he were stuck in the paradigm of the Red Queen. No matter how fast he ran, the Faunling remained beyond his reach.

Then, one night, Dom gave up trying to reach the little being. He considered that maybe this creature wasn't for him; perhaps the Faunling had another purpose altogether. So he sat down in a field of crown vetch several feet away, staring over the budded heads of purple at the Faunling.

The wildflowers danced on a breeze that tickled the hair around Dom's ears. For a moment he looked away from the little creature, off to his right, where the field's edge faded into the wall of a towering forest. Deep vibrations rumbled underneath Dom as if something bigger and stronger walked nearby, hiding in the trees. Fear lodged in his chest, freezing his lungs mid-breath. Since childhood, Dom had the uncanny ability to detach from the dream world to rouse himself awake. However, he tended to do this when his dreams toed the border into the realm of nightmares. For whatever reason, this time he couldn't do that.

Whatever walked in the forest stopped moving in the trees across from Dom.

Three iridescent purple eyes stared back at him from a dark hollow inside the tree line and up in the canopy. Two sat side by side with the third above, straddling the lower two. Whispers of a language strange to his ears drifted across the field. It was no known language that Dom could pinpoint. While fluent in a couple of languages, from Spanish to Czech, he shuddered at its foreignness. It was a language that could be extinct or . . . alien.

Hypnotized, he stared at the three eyes. They were all he could discern of the giant being through the trees. His mind went into a programming mode of sorts. Organic and inorganic formulas downloaded and swirled about the white space in his brain. An idea developed: a recipe for new life.

Pressure on his right knee shattered the letters, numbers, and symbols, raining them down in a jumbled pile of chaos that evaporated as his vision returned to his present place in the dream. The three eyes in the forest were gone. Dom looked down to see the Faunling before him, its dainty paw on his leg, deep blue eyes, wide as saucers, reflecting the stars above.

"Hello," it said.

Dom sat up so violently in bed that his head snapped forward. A pop sounded in his neck. His wife, Marilla, screamed. Her cries woke baby Viktor, asleep in a bassinet near Marilla's side.

"Mother Mary!" Marilla's hand grasped Dom's shoulder. "What's wrong?"

He reached to touch her hand, but she withdrew it as she turned her attention to the wailing Viktor.

Shaken and needing comfort, Dom shook his heavy head in the darkened bedroom. Marilla's weight lifted from her side of the mattress as she went to Viktor in his bassinet. Before Dom knew it, she had Viktor in her arms, singing and cooing at him.

A spark of jealousy lit in Dom's chest. He tossed the covers off more violently than needed and headed downstairs for a glass of water.

Aside from the soft footsteps of Marilla walking the baby around the bedroom above, the house stood silent. No noise stirred from Aria's room. She'd slept through the commotion.

The ice water stung Dom's mouth and throat as he gulped it down. As he became more conscious, the formulas from his dream began to piece themselves together once more. He needed to write them down. They meant something. He refilled his glass and took it with him to the basement.

Aside from the hot water tank and the furnace, his office commandeered the whole space. A giant whiteboard covered the longest wall. Dom grabbed four dry-erase markers off his desk, each a different color. Then, in his chicken-scratch handwriting, he wrote out everything he could remember of the formula from his dream.

The glass of water had grown lukewarm by the time Dom finished scribbling. He used his cell phone to take a photo of the colorful formula.

This formula was it. It was what Dom had been trying to develop during his twenty years in genetics. Dom was confident this formula would generate a new and intelligent species. It'd only taken one night to make his dreams come true.

———

"Thanks for the help with the baby."

Dom cringed at the venomous tone in his wife's voice.

She faced the sink, away from him, as he came up the basement stairs. The hexagonal-shaped virtual assistant sitting on the kitchen counter next to the coffeepot displayed the time as 8:00 a.m. He'd never returned to the bedroom after waking.

Marilla turned with a plate full of bacon and sausage in her hand. Pancakes cooked on the griddle behind her. "Had I known that your scientist brain would interrupt my sleep for the rest of my life, I might have reconsidered my life choices."

"But then I wouldn't be here, Mommy," Aria said.

Dom smiled at his daughter. Always the sharp one, even at six years old.

"You still would have been," Marilla said, low enough for Aria to miss.

Aria was one of his greatest accomplishments. Mirella continually dismissed her.

Dom hadn't chosen wisely with Marilla, but he'd needed a woman who wouldn't ask questions and could provide a home for him and Aria. However, now that she lived a life of luxury, she believed herself in control of the household, resulting in a growing superiority complex. Dom didn't like it. But he said nothing and just sat down to breakfast. The best thing about Mirella was that she could cook.

"Hi, Daddy!" Aria squeaked as he sat down next to her at the island counter. She worked on math homework during breakfast. Mirella hated that. She didn't believe a child should always be working or studying. But Aria wanted to be just like her daddy when she grew up. He snapped a mental picture of her lovely, beaming face.

She scraped the pancakes off the griddle and split the stack onto two plates. The smaller stack she placed in front of Aria; the larger stack she walked around the kitchen island to Dom. As she slid the plate before him, she leaned in and whispered in his ear. "It's no wonder your first wife left you. And the only way she could escape from you was by dying."

Sharp cuts in his hands stung, formed by his fingernails from clenching his fist tight. An ache in his jaw raced toward his left ear as he ground his teeth.

"Mommy, I would like some syrup, please," Aria asked.

"You know where it's at." Marilla turned her back on them and went upstairs. Aria slid off the tall chair and went over to the refrigerator.

"Maaa-aaa-aaa!" Viktor stood against the wall of the playpen that Dom had gotten him on his first birthday last month, banging away at the side with a plastic teething ring. It wasn't the typical "Pack-and-play" sort of pen but three-foot-long, three-foot-high plastic latticelike squares that, when the seven sides were connected, formed a heptagonal play area where Viktor could have free rein within a small space.

Marilla ignored his wails and went upstairs. A fire ignited in Dom's stomach with his anger. She had no right to speak ill of his deceased first wife. Though she wasn't entirely wrong. All the women in Dom's life left him. His mother left him behind after she died of leukemia. Then his *tía* took him in. But when she learned that the monthly stipend she'd get from the state to care for Dom wouldn't cover the cost of having an extra mouth to feed, she handed him over to the state. A foster home saw Dom grow through his adolescence and teenage years, and he stayed in the same house despite the influx of kids who came and went. The other kids tended to avoid him, thinking he was weird and different. Dom sought comfort in books and learning new things. Despite never having a stable family life, he managed to be top of his class and received a full scholarship to MIT.

He'd met Ellie four years after he graduated with his PhD in genetics. She'd been everything he'd wanted in a woman. And he was everything she needed. Or so he thought.

A sharp prick on his forearm elicited a yelp from Dom as he slid to the right of his chair, a reaction to flee. Aria giggled so hard that her tiny pearl-white teeth and rosy gums were completely visible. She looked at him, bright blue eyes sparkling from the excitement of scaring him.

She'd stabbed him with her syrup-dipped fork.

"Aria!"

She giggled. "Want some syrup, Daddy?"

Dom looked down at her plate. Two tiny pancakes floated in a sticky amber sea. He picked up the beige bottle with a big red maple leaf printed on its front. He'd bought the bottle at a turnpike rest stop on his way to NYC last year. Now, whatever remained of the maple syrup filled Aria's plate. She licked her fork and ran it through her syrup pond before licking it again.

Marilla would have a fit with this mess, but Dom didn't care. Marilla never truly mattered to him, nor was she what he wanted. This relationship probably is an echo of how things would have gone with Ellie if she hadn't abandoned him by dying in a car accident a few months after she gave him the only thing he'd ever wanted (aside from the life-creating genetic formula): Aria, the only female presence he needed in his life.

"Let me have some of that." He picked up Aria's plate and poured syrup onto his stack of pancakes.

"Careful, Daddy!"

"I'm always careful, kiddo." He scooped some bacon and sausage onto his plate and dove in.

There was a tug at his T-shirt sleeve. He turned to Aria. She looked up at him wide-eyed.

"What 'speriments were you doing in the basement all night?" she whispered, knowing full well that what he did in the basement was a secret. Dom wanted to correct her that the word was "experiments," but this was part of her innocence; he didn't want to take that away from her. He never wanted her to grow up. Aria was at the perfect age.

"Oh," he whispered back to her before folding a strip of bacon into his mouth. "It's going to be an amazing surprise."

"Will I love it?"

He beamed at her. Aria was going to love what he had in store. Dom smiled as he chewed and savored the bacon in his mouth. The *world* was going to love what he had in store.

———

The pudu, a small South American deer, best resembled the body of the Faunling. Since the night of their first contact during his dreams, he and the creature had sat for hours under the night sky in the crown vetch field, just staring at each other. He never again saw the three-eyed creature that haunted the forest.

He wanted the creature to be disease-resistant, so he incorporated DNA from a few species of sharks. For the coloration and texture of the fur, Dom used the genes from a domesticated Bengal house cat. He also tried to incorporate the cat's agility and speed. A bit of a deviation from the Faunling of his dreams, but he wanted something that could escape any predator. Plus, the fur coloration would draw in a more bougie crowd.

Dom had a few other mammalian genes lined up to add, but he thought better of it this round; he wanted to see how this first version developed.

He laughed. "Faunlings will be the next level of designer pets created by Thenurgee!"

"Think of it," Dom said to his new CEO, "a cuddly little animal with the intelligence of a chimp who can speak and swiftly evade predators—or a car. The Faunling is the ultimate house pet. They're resistant to disease and aging, thanks to shark DNA. Hell, they may outlive their owners. Plus, the Faunling will be smart enough to stay home or not get lost if it goes outside."

Basil Waddington sat behind his mahogany desk, fingers tented before his nose. The man wore gold-framed ear-hooked glasses despite their being decades out of style. Waddington had taken over the company after the previous CEO (and Dom's best friend), Sebastian Blatt, had been murdered along with his second wife and their son. Rumor was that the family returned home one night and surprised a pair of burglars. After Sebastian's death, Waddington had promoted Dom to chief scientist officer. The best perk of his new title was a lab of his own. It took up the entire fourteenth floor of the Thenurgee headquarters.

"We'll corner the market for those with mental health issues who need an emotional support animal." Dom looked at the creature, and it looked back. Warmth flushed through him as he thought about the wonder and intelligence that emanated from the little animal.

"It will talk. And let's face it . . ." Dom scratched the Faunling's chin. It made a sound between a coo and a purr. ". . . it's irresistibly adorable."

Waddington stared at the creature.

"What do you say?" Dom smiled at his boss.

Waddington placed his hands flat on his desk and stared at the Faunling. The creature shuddered and looked back up at Dom— concern filling its eyes. Dom bit his lip. He grew nervous, and the Faunling's concerned look intensified.

"Well, this is version One-dot-oh," Dom stammered on, realizing that Waddington didn't quite believe the Faunling would one day be able to talk. "The next version will talk. My attempt to incorporate the African gray parrot genes did not synthesize properly, causing the anatomical structure and intelligence required to control speech not to work as expected in this version. Might need to add in something else—"

Waddington cleared his throat and pushed himself back in his chair, which gave a piercing squeak with the movement.

The Faunling flinched. Dom ran his hand down its back to calm it.

"Blatt did right in keeping you on for as long as he did," Waddington finally spoke. Dom looked down, hurt at the comment because he had been Sebastian's "behind-the-scenes right-hand man." He and Sebastian, best friends since their MIT days, had been the ones to establish Thenurgee and invent the company's initial line of revenue: Build-a-Baby, a product that enabled parents to build—with whatever specifications they dreamed—their own child. For years the product had been Thenurgee's most lucrative product, until a defect became evident in all the children. One swept under the rug, and the whole Build-a-Baby line had come to a screeching halt after the horrific murder of Sebastian's first wife. He had helped Sebastian cover everything up—including the child that Sebastian had built for his wife, who was her ultimate killer. Sebastian would have never gotten rid of Dom; he was the science and the keeper of secrets behind Thenurgee.

"I get the sense that you want to try something the lawyers may not agree with," Waddington said.

Dom kept his hand on the back of One-dot-oh and his eyes on the ground.

Waddington continued: "Why do you think Sebastian had you become CSO in his will? He believed in you and what you'll do for the future of humanity, no matter the cost." Waddington gave Dom a sinister smile. "Whatever you do for the next version, keep it off the books."

———

Dom's good spirits that evening weren't the slightest bit dampened by the three suitcases next to the front door. Not even the sight of Aria clinging to Viktor while Marilla tried to pry their son out of his daughter's arms could shatter his good mood.

"What's going on here?" he chuckled.

Marilla stood, red-faced, and smoothed back the fly-aways that had come loose from her tightly pinned bun.

"Dominik. Viktor and I are leaving." The matter-of-fact way she said this made it sound rehearsed.

Aria burst into tears. Dom, ignoring what Marilla said, went to his children. He smiled at Aria and held out his hands. His daughter placed her brother in his arms.

"You're making a big mistake here." The smile on his face spread until the corners of his lips couldn't pull any further away from each other.

"The only mistake I made was staying this long and having a kid with you." Marilla snatched Viktor from Dom.

"Daddy, no!" Aria screamed. "Don't let her take him."

"Sweetie, she's his mother; let them go."

Allowing Marilla to leave with Viktor would be a godsend. She'd just been a marriage of convenience anyways. Now that he made enough money, he could pay someone to care for both the house and Aria.

"Daddy . . ." Tears welled up in Aria's bright blue eyes.

He got down on his knees before her. "You and me; we only need each other from now on."

"Oh, please." Marilla rolled her eyes and then jumped at the sound of heavy knocks at the front door. With baby Viktor in her arms, she turned to open it.

A man, about ten years younger than Marilla and looking like the kind of guy who spends far too much time bench-pressing at the gym, waited on the other side. Although taller and much fitter than Dom, this new guy visibly shuddered when they locked eyes. Marilla was leaving him for good. And he didn't care. Everything he needed was here in front of him—and in a cage at his Thenurgee lab.

Despite this, a touch of sadness invaded Dom's thoughts. Just like all the other women in his life, now Marilla was leaving him too—abandoning him for a muscle head. As for Aria . . . Well, it was inevitable that she'd leave him one day. A void formed in his chest and spread to his heart at this thought. He had the urge to grab Aria and hold her close, to wrap his arms around her tiny self, crack open his ribs, and place her inside him, consuming her to fill the void.

"Just you and me, kiddo." He grimaced as he pushed down the dark thoughts. *Focus on this moment*, he thought while touching Aria's shoulder to get her attention away from her stepmother, who she so desperately wanted as a mommy, and the baby brother she'd dreamed of.

———

"You're going to lose her," the Faunling in his lap said as they sat beside the pond.

The crown vetch swayed in the breeze. Since Marilla left, Dom's dreams had become cooler and windier.

"Aria won't leave me," Dom growled, not quite believing his own words.

The sky above them darkened as each star began to wink out.

"It is inevitable. All little girls grow up and leave their daddies."

"Not my Aria."

"Life is changing."

"Not always. I know how to keep Aria from growing up. How to keep her with me forever."

———

"Want a marshmallow, Daddy?" Aria shoveled a spoonful of frosted cereal and dehydrated marshmallows into her mouth.

Dom leaned against the counter and looked at her, hunched over her unicorn bowl, scooping colorful cereal into her tiny mouth with her R2-D2 spoon. He snapped a mental picture of this scene, never to forget how happy she looked. He needed to remember how she looked; it was the only way he could control the newly formed void in his chest that gnawed to the emptiness it fed.

Dom stood up straight, stretched, and clapped his hands. "Want to go on an adventure tonight after school?"

Aria hopped off the stool, ran around the kitchen island, and wrapped her small, thin arms around his quads. "Yes, oh yes, oh yes!" Her long brown curls bounced in tune with her excitement as she squealed. Then she stepped back and whispered, "Where are we going?"

Dom took her by her shoulders. She giggled with glee. "It's a surprise, kiddo. Now get ready for school. The bus will be here in thirty minutes."

———

Dom stayed home that day and reran the algorithms for the final step in perfecting the Faunling's formula. He figured out what kept One-dot-oh from developing the right vocal cords. It needed genes from a more complex and intelligent organism.

The front door slammed shut, and squeals of "Daaaaaaddddyyyy" traveled across the floorboards above, along with the tiny running

156

footsteps of a child making directly for the basement stairs. Aria was there before he could get up, jumping like a springer spaniel next to him. Her pink and purple star–splashed backpack bounced with her movements.

"Where are we going? Can we go now?" she repeated while jumping.

Dom laughed and placed a hand on his chest while slowly exhaling. The void quivered and grew cold in his chest. "Go change out of your school uniform and into some comfy clothes—whatever you want. Want to get a cheeseburger kids' meal for dinner?"

Her right arm shot into the air, hand balled into a fist. "Yes!" And with that, she bolted back up the stairs.

———

"Can I please play with her?" Aria asked while sitting on one of the lab's swiveling chairs. She twisted it back and forth, pushing a slippered foot against his desk.

Dom smiled as he filled a syringe with a greenish-orange serum he'd just synthesized. "No, you can't play with it now."

One-dot-oh, who sat in the cage off to Dom's left, chirped and looked at Aria. Its small deerlike tail wagged in what Dom believed to be a display of happiness or excitement.

"Aw, but she's so cute. I want to hug her." Aria leaned forward to get off the chair.

Dom gave her the sternest look any father could give a daughter dressed in dinosaur-costume pajamas with a frilled hood that made her look like a pink *Dilophosaurus* from *Jurassic Park*. "Don't move your little dinosaur butt from that spot. And finish your fries." She'd taken his direction to dress comfortably quite literally. Dom was grateful that only the ancient, senile guard stood duty tonight on his floor. No one else saw him come in with a pink dinosaur.

157

Aria sat back in the chair, crossed her arms, and gave her cold fries a disgusted look. "I'm bored and want to play."

The Faunling chirped at Aria and pawed at the bars. Dom reached into its cage and patted its head to calm it down. It was nervous. He was nervous too.

"No fair!" she cried as she saw Dom pet the creature.

"Go sit on the sofa, and I'll let you hold it." Dom capped and pocketed the syringe before taking the Faunling from the cage. The rhythm of his heartbeat throbbed in his ears, and the void inside his ribcage hummed, muffling the room's sound.

Aria was off the chair and sitting on the sofa before he could turn with the animal in hand.

"Excited?" he chuckled. Aria smiled underneath her dinosaur hood. Dom took another mental picture of her. The Faunling shivered in his hands.

He sat next to Aria and placed the creature in her lap. Ever so gently, she wrapped her arms around it in a soft embrace and nuzzled her face against the side of its head.

"You're the cutest thing ever," she whispered.

The Faunling chirped in response. It pulled its head away to stare wide-eyed at Dom, then back to Aria. Sweat formed on Dom's neck and back as a spark of fear lit in his chest. He wondered if the creature knew what he was about to do.

As Aria continued to coo at the Faunling, Dom slipped the syringe from his pocket, uncapped it, and jabbed the needle through the fabric of Aria's dinosaur pajamas—emptying the vial's contents into the meaty part of her upper arm.

The Faunling screeched and jumped off Aria, disappearing into the lab. Aria looked at Dom, surprise and pain etched on her face—and what Dom assumed to be a look of betrayal. Tears filled her eyes as her pupils dilated, consuming the blue of her irises. A strand of drool dripped from the corner of her mouth as her eyes rolled back in her head. She fell face forward toward his lap, but he caught her and rolled her to her back. Aria let out one long exhalation.

Dom scooped her up in his arms. Pulling back her hood, he buried his nose in her curls, breathing in the scent of strawberry shampoo and Aria. The void beat at his ribcage, ravenously aching with need and fear.

The sofa creaked as he stood with Aria in his arms. Dom looked down upon the unconscious angelic face of his firstborn—now his greatest invention—and didn't take a mental picture of her.

———

The crown vetch field turned brown underneath the fading moon and missing stars. The Faunling faced Dom, keeping a level of separation from him. A tear of blood trickled out of its left eye. The sight caused Dom's stomach to sour—the cold air of his dreamworld bit into his skin.

"You're still going to lose her," it said.

———

Aria's screams shattered Dom's nightmare. One-dot-oh, who he'd found cowering under his desk, howled from its cage and pawed between the bars at Aria's writhing form. Her screams grew in shrillness and volume. One-dot-oh soon matched her tone.

Dom fell off the sofa and crawled over to Aria's cage, which was conjoined with One-dot-oh's. He punched in the access code several times with sweaty fingers before he had the right combination. The barred door swung open, and Dom watched his only daughter writhe on her back atop a sticky, orange-oozed-covered floor. Aria's arms shot straight up with a cracking sound that Dom knew he'd never forget. She screeched as her clawed fingers turned black and shriveled. Her tiny fingers fell off one by one and landed on the floor in a pile of withered bone and flesh.

The loud pop of her knees bending in the opposite direction caused bile to rise and burn Dom's throat. He did all he could to hold down his dinner of an onion-slathered cheeseburger with a side of fries as the stench of shit and piss washed over him. The orange ooze turned to a bloody, watery mulch beneath Aria.

"Daaaaaaaaaa. Daaaaaaaa," gargled from her mouth as her eyes rolled sideways in their sockets to look at him. Tears wept across the upper crest of her left cheek, down the side of her face, and pooled in the well of her elongated ear.

Terror. All Dom could see was terror on her face. He leaned into the cage, arm extended toward her. One-dot-oh snarled and swiped at him between the bars, drawing blood on the back of his hand. Shocked, Dom fell backward and looked at the Faunling—its eyes black, lips curled, exposing sharp canines that Dom never realized it had. It hovered on the other side of the bars near Aria's head and glowered at Dom. He closed the door to Aria's cage as she continued to gurgle, "Daaaaaaaa. Daaaaaaa."

Dom couldn't look at her as she began to shrink inside her blood-stained pajamas. He threw a blanket over her cage then covered his ears to drown out the sounds of her bones popping—contorting her into her new shape—and her screams.

———

Soft sounds of crying and comforting words of "It's okay. I'm okay" came from underneath the blanket. Dom listened to his daughter's words and the soft cooing from One-dot-oh. He pulled the blanket away.

Aria, or what was once Aria, lay curled against the bars that separated her and One-dot-oh. Through the bars, it petted her head with its paw.

"Aria?" Dom crawled toward the cage's door.

She lifted her head from her furry front legs. Dom tried to gulp as his mouth went dry. Aria looked exactly like One-dot-oh except for two differences: Her face was still human—still Aria—and her fur was a luminous white. So brilliantly white that she almost seemed to glow inside the cage.

His hypothesis that the human genome was the missing key to enabling the Faunling to speak had been confirmed. The quickest way to test the theory had been to create a serum to turn humans into Faunlings. Now he knew what to do to develop the next version.

Dom coughed into his hand, trying to cover up the smile that pulled at the corner of his lips. In addition to his finding, he'd ensured that his daughter would be safe with him forever. She'd never have to worry about getting sick or growing old in this new form. He'd never have to worry about losing her.

"Daddy, why?" Her eyes shimmered with tears as she looked at him.

"My baby. It's just you and me. Forever."

Aria wailed.

———

"Sir!" Dom, disheveled, pushed past Waddington's secretary and barged into his CEO's office.

"What is the meaning of this?" Waddington looked at Dom from head to toe, a disgusted look crossing his face.

"It's a success. Two-dot-oh is a success."

Waddington's face changed; a smile broke out, one Dom had never seen before. It didn't look right on his normally scowling face. "Great. Bring it in."

"Ah, sir, she's having trouble . . . um . . . adapting to her new life. Can I bring her to you in a week? I fear stressing her out by meeting new people could make her sick."

The sour expression returned to Waddington's face. He moved his mouth as though chewing on something bitter. "She? Her? And these things aren't supposed to get sick."

"Yes, sir. It's a girl—I mean, female. I said they were disease-resistant. They can still experience symptoms from stress and anxiety."

Waddington seemed to contemplate his words. "Fine, bring her to me once she's settled. And it's really a female?"

"Yes, sir. She is. Two-dot-oh is a good little girl."

———

Dom spent the next few days trying to get Two-dot-oh stable. She'd taken to biting Dom or calling him nasty names like "butthead" every time he attempted to get close to her. Then she'd tell him she hated him or that she would run away. On top of that, One-dot-oh would go berserk whenever he got near Two-dot-oh.

Maybe if he took Two-dot-oh to his home lab, she'd calm down in a familiar area. Plus, locking her in the basement would be more secure. Too many people had keys to his lab. At home, it would just be the two of them.

Dom tranquilized Two-dot-oh for transport. As she was still a tiny creature—smaller than One-dot-oh, it was easy to sneak her home via a document box.

At home, he set up Viktor's playpen in the basement to give Two-dot-oh room to walk around versus being stuck in a tiny cage. Dom would spend his days in his basement office working, while Two-dot-oh slept most of the day curled in the furthest corner away from him in her new habitat. Dom tried to talk to her, but she ignored him. At night, when he attempted to tuck her in the little bed he'd built for her, she tried to bite him. Dom gave up having any physical contact with her. He let her sleep wherever she wanted inside the pen while he sat outside to read her bedtime stories.

Nights were the loneliest. The big house stood silent and still. The walls no longer echoed with Aria's sweet voice or laughter. He missed holding his daughter in his arms. If Dom sedated her, he could hold her on the couch while he watched television—just like he used to. Though Dom couldn't bring himself to do that. The thought of tranquilizing Two-dot-oh flashed in his mind. He knew that if he started down that road, he wouldn't stop. And who knew what the long-term effects came from tranquilizing a Faunling?

Dom couldn't sate the hunger of the void inside him, and he feared sleeping. The Faunling in his dreams no longer provided helpful information that could progress the growth of future Faunling versions. No, now all the Faunling did was provide warnings—warnings that Two-dot-oh would leave him and he'd be forever alone.

His hands shook as he worried about his creation leaving him. He'd poured his whole life into her; the thought of her abandoning him like every other woman in his life. . .. No, he couldn't let that happen. He'd never allow Two-dot-oh to leave him.

"It's getting harder to contain you," he whispered as he sat hunched on the floor while looking at Two-dot-oh, who snarled at him from underneath his desk. Her white fur sparkled an iridescent blue from the LED lights on his surge protector, and the little light gave him clear visibility of the sharp teeth she had in her mouth. It wouldn't do to have vicious teeth like that on a commercial product. Dom could already envision lawsuits from bites. He'd need to fix that at some point.

Behind him, the inner plastic wall of the playpen lay in bits. Two-dot-oh had chewed through it during the night and wreaked havoc on his office—though she couldn't reach the top of the desk, so his computer had been spared. The carpet, cabinets, and walls were another matter. There were claw and chew marks everywhere. And the overwhelming smell of urine let Dom know that Two-dot-oh had pissed all over the place.

She'd figured out how to escape her enclosure. When she figured out how to open doors, she'd be gone, just like all the other females in his life.

He'd thought that turning his daughter into a Faunling would keep her with him forever. Instead, it had caused her to hate him with a passion he never imagined his daughter could have. Dom had to do something about this. A growling hunger rumbled in his chest as he ran his hands through his thinning hair—a hunger fueled by fear of more loss.

Dom stood and went to the closet; the bottom corner of the door was newly chewed through. There he found the pet carrier Marilla had for her prized domestic Bengal cat before it had mysteriously run away last year. He paused, smiling for a moment to remember how morose she had been when she realized the cat wasn't coming home. Dom had convinced her that Sir Poppins had probably been hit by a car. She didn't need to know that some of Sir Poppins' DNA had helped build One-dot-oh and Two-dot-oh's bodies.

Two-dot-oh jumped out from underneath the desk when Dom turned around, cat carrier in hand. Her fur stood on end, and saliva dripped from her open, teeth-bared mouth. Dom pinched the clasp on the metal gate door and opened it, then took a few tentative steps forward. Two-dot-oh, still snarling, sidestepped toward the basement stairs—a fruitless effort because the door at the top was shut.

Dom set the carrier down, keeping its door open. Before Two-dot-oh could react, he jumped forward and, keeping an arm's distance away, grabbed her by the back scruff of her neck. She yowled, snapping her teeth in vain at his forearm. As he whipped her toward the carrier, she swung with enough momentum to swipe a hind claw and tear through his white shirt at his stomach.

The stinging sensation shot up his chest, burning through the pounding void and infuriating him. He grabbed the carrier, tipped it back, and threw her in. Her small form easily slipped through the doorway, and she let out a squeak of pain as she slammed into the back of the carrier. Dom slammed the metal gate shut and locked the clasp in place. Then he dropped the carrier to the floor.

As he stood, he nearly kicked the carrier across the room in anger, but the crying from the carrier stirred memories of his Aria crying whenever she fell, skinned a knee, or cut a finger. Dom's heart broke at the thought of how poorly he had treated Two-dot-oh.

"Daddy, you hurt me," Two-dot-oh said, her bright eyes looking at him through the airholes on the carrier's side. Dom touched his stomach and felt the pain from the scratches. The void hummed and ached with emptiness. Dom swallowed the lump in his throat, turned, and ran up the stairs.

"Please don't leave me alone here," Two-dot-oh wailed from the carrier on the floor in the center of the basement. Dom turned off the lights, opened the basement door, and walked into the afternoon-lit kitchen. He locked the door behind him before going upstairs to shower and clean his wounds.

———

"You'll lose her," the Faunling said; but for Dom, tonight was different. He lay on the couch in the living room and looked out into the kitchen at the creature. Dom had camped out all day watching television and even planned to sleep there to hear if Two-dot-oh escaped the carrier and tried to get through the basement door. Dom had not returned to the basement since he put Two-dot-oh in the carrier. He couldn't bring himself to see her. To see what he had done to her. Now and again, her faint cries would travel up the stairs and could be heard on the house's first floor, but Dom would turn up the television volume to drown out the cries.

Dom got up from the couch and walked out into the kitchen. The Faunling sat atop the island counter, chastising him. "You deserve to."

Dom shook his head. He didn't deserve that. Two-dot-oh must stay with him forever. The void within Dom woke at that thought and growled with an empty hunger. The Faunling shivered, the fleshy appendages on its head quivering with the movement.

Dom walked past the creature, opened the basement door, flicked on the lights, and went to his office. Two-dot-oh slept on the carpeted floor at the foot of the stairs. She'd broken out of the carrier. Anger filled Dom's belly at her continued attempts to leave him. He was going to make sure she never left him again.

Before Two-dot-oh could fully wake, Dom was on top of her. She squealed as he gripped her upper body in his hands. Her hind legs flailed as she tried to claw him.

"Daddy!" Two-dot-oh screamed.

The words didn't register. Dom just stared at Two-dot-oh's face, the angelic face that looked so much like his daughter's. Oh, how he missed his Aria. His stomach growled again.

"Let me go!"

Dom knew precisely how to keep his Aria with him forever. If she lived inside of him, he could keep her forever. Aria could never abandon him. She needed to become a part of him.

Aria used to sing when she was making art, "Somewhere Over the Rainbow." She'd sing as she filled her drawings with brilliant colors and the air with lyrics about escaping.

Dom played the memory of her singing to drown out her high-pitched screams as he bit into Two-dot-oh's neck and tore away a large chunk of flesh.

Rivulets of blood poured from the wound, over his hands, onto the floor. Two-dot-oh's eyes went wide as she thrashed. He squeezed her chest while her front paws beat at his forearms. The popping sound of ribs cracking didn't break his trance, nor did the blood that burst from her mouth, splattering across his face.

"Daddy," a raspy wheeze of Two-dot-oh's voice dripped from her bloody mouth.

Dom chewed the flesh he'd torn away and swallowed, still hearing Aria's light voice singing in his memory. Two-dot-oh's lips went slack, and she looked at him with dark eyes. The brilliant blue sparkle dulled as her pupils fluctuated in erratic patterns.

Two-dot-oh's body went limp as he tore into the soft flesh of her belly and began to consume her from the inside out.

———

Dom sat up. His lungs burned. He couldn't stop screaming from the horrific nightmare. He looked around his office for something to break his panic. But it wasn't something he could see that interrupted his attack. It was something he felt in the palm of his hand. Something warm, like a tiny hand being held in his own.

Aria. His heartbeat slowed, and the constant ache of the void in his chest was gone. Aria had returned to him. She'd finally allowed him to hold her, comforting him as he suffered through that horrific dream.

His eyes adjusted to the light of the basement, and he looked down to find himself sitting in a pool of blood. Dom squeezed what was in his hand, resisting the urge to look at it. Whatever it was, it wasn't big enough to be Aria. He exhaled and gathered the courage to bring whatever he held to his face.

Dom screamed as he uncurled his fingers and saw the tiny, bloodied Faunling paw in his hand.

We Still Have Time

Present Day . . . twenty-one hours remaining

We're barricaded, by our own volition, in my living unit, separated from the rest of the *Parallax*. The makeshift calendar Tyler made from outdated hydro-unit schematics tracks how long we've isolated ourselves. The space station's auxiliary power has kept us alive so far. Once that runs out, we're dead, stranded at the edge of the Kuiper Belt. We no longer keep our InfoComm units charged to salvage each precious watt and are therefore oblivious to the actual time aside from what Tyler's calendar tells us. Tyler believes we have a few weeks of electricity remaining—if we're lucky. Neither of us steps foot outside of my quarters anymore unless we're scrounging for food or supplies. When we do, one goes alone with protection and extreme caution. The other stays behind to keep watch on the only door into the oblivion, ensuring nothing slips inside.

Tyler returns from a food run. We can only carry so much at one time or we would have cleared out the canteen by now. We should find a cart but agreed to not go out of our way to look for one. It's too dangerous and takes too much time to deviate from the path directly to the canteen. Bags are out of the question because you never know what else they may carry.

I keep watch as he steps through the doorway, ensuring that nothing follows him over the threshold. After closing the door, he unzips the pouch sewn into the waist of his spacewalk suit and pulls out several meat source and pasta puree packets, setting them on my desk. Without a hello, he takes off the suit and helmet, hanging both on the peg next to the bathroom door.

We don't trust the door's locking mechanism, since we believe the entire ship's been compromised—given the main power never came back online—and after Tyler performs his manual override on the door, locking it, we slide the couch up against it for extra protection.

As we push the sofa into place, my knee gives out.

"Whoa there," Tyler says, catching me before I hit the floor. I smile before righting myself and continue helping him with the sofa. Once in place, he turns to me. "You okay?"

"Yeah, just tweaked my knee wrong when I pushed." A lie. I don't want him to know what happened. It's better if I just disappear.

Tomorrow I'll tell him I need tampons and go out on a "supply run." He'll think it strange because he just went out and I should've said something to him, but the mention of tampons will leave him red and silent. My excuse. We've been together for over six years, involved before we chose to go on this mission, and he still cannot bring himself to touch a box of tampons. In reality, I'll be going off somewhere to die. He doesn't need to know I'm infested. Tyler will kill me on the spot, and I don't want that on his conscience.

Running away gives Tyler more time before he is infested as well ... or eaten.

———

Almost Three Months Ago . . . 2,189 hours remaining

"Space does odd things to one's genes," Dr. Isabella Miriam said, her head bent low over a tray as she pipetted a bluish liquid.

"I thought they discredited that seventy years ago with Scott Kelly, when his genes were only temporarily affected by space's environment." I snapped shut a casing clasp on the water filter under Dr. Miriam's lab sink. She said nothing but cracked a crooked, toothy smile. I yawned and looked at my watch: 7:30 a.m. I hated it when she played games this early in the morning. "Right?"

She raised her head slightly, never taking her eyes off the tray in front of her. "Sure."

The woman unsettled me. I disliked living so close to the lab because I saw her every morning. She stood behind one of the lab's large bay windows watching us—the ones who kept the ship running—pass by as if we were a colony of little ants. Her own specimens. Dull red lips pinched in the corners. Her light-colored, almost translucent, eyes moving rapidly as she set her sights on each one of us. I hated her; yet, at the same time, she fascinated me. Which is why I tended to volunteer for the tasks in her lab. No one else wanted the work, and I had to know what she was tinkering with in there.

"What's the latest project?" I asked and closed the cabinet.

Her shoulders shook twice as a soft giggle escaped her lips, then murmured, "Things and stuff."

She was being secretive. Did the commander know what kind of experiments she was doing in here? Had he sanctioned them? On the opposite side of the room, a wall of terrariums lined inset shelves. Each held some type of insect that Dr. Miriam had brought with her from Earth: praying mantis, rhinoceros beetles, walking sticks, etc. The terrariums were filled with substrate conducive to each insect's lifestyle. However, there was one that was devoid of anything but the air inside and about ten flies. All they could do was fly or walk on the glass walls. They were beautiful. No bigger than a nickel, their wings caught the light in a cascade of rainbow colors. Their eyes were a brilliant turquoise and sat atop long thin stalks that connected to a soft pink head and body. A far cry from the typical dull, red-eyed housefly.

"Where'd these come from? I've never seen flies like this before," I asked since they were not in her lab last week.

A toothy smile stretched across her face as she finally looked at me, laugh lines cracking the corners of her eyes. "Those are my babies."

"Your babies?"

"Yes."

"They look weird." I shuddered. Bugs are gross. "Little rainbow nightmares."

With my fingernail, I tapped the terrarium's glass. The vibration sent them all into flight. They whirled about each other in a circle around the interior of the terrarium, like horses racing at the track back on Earth. Their wings caught the bright lights of the lab and sparkled like little multicolored jewels. I was torn between hating them for their buggish appearance and being entranced by their colors.

"What species are they?" I asked.

She returned her focus to her pipette and tray, a signal that she no longer wanted to talk. I wasn't going to get anything further from her.

—

"I tell you, she's like Dr. Frankenstein in there. Creating her own . . . things," I told Tyler.

We lay in my bed. He arrived twenty minutes ago after a seventeen-hour shift working on the master radio communication unit's electrical panel, which had gone on the fritz yesterday.

He rolled over, away from me. I hadn't seen him since he left at six that morning. "Annie, just let me sleep. Can you tell me all about it in the morning?"

I turned my back to him in a silent huff, allowing the tears to slide down my cheek and wet my pillow. After six years, this was our relationship. Work apart all day, barely speak when together at night. Love still existed strongly between us; I could see it in his eyes and feel it in my heart. Maybe Tyler was right when, a few nights ago, he said the time had come to return to our home in Pennsylvania.

A pang of homesickness caught in my throat. He was right; the time had come to go home. I missed our condo that sat at the edge of the Pocono Mountains. Our large living room window overlooked the forest. Luckily, the view of the urban sprawl that spread north from Philadelphia through Allentown and on toward NYC was blocked by the apartment behind us. I prayed that, despite our being gone all these years, our view from our little home remained unchanged.

A faint blue emanated from the light strip recessed around the ceiling molding. It began to pulsate ever so slightly. I'd forgotten to turn it off before I crawled under the covers and wasn't about to get up and do so now. Most wouldn't have noticed the faint pulsation, but being in the maintenance sector as long as I have, you notice the little things. One of the nuclear generators was kicking into overdrive.

In a few moments, the light went still. Someone switched the reactors, giving the active one a rest before it had a meltdown. Always on the brink of a cataclysm in space. The tiniest thing could kill you. Even something as small as a nick in your spacesuit while on a spacewalk.

I fell asleep to thoughts of Dr. Miriam creating monsters in her lab.

———

"Annie! Get up!" Tyler shook my shoulders. A siren screeched from the hallway.

It was our day off, and I wanted to sleep in. Groggily, I collected my senses and stared wide-eyed at him. The auxiliary lights were on; the blue strip lights weren't.

"What's going on?

"I don't know, but there's a ton of yelling and screaming in the hallway." He ran over to my couch. "Get up and help me slide this in front of the door. The lock may be compromised."

I threw off the covers and ran over, the coldness of the floor sending a shock through my feet and legs.

Tyler must've seen my confusion at the cold, unheated floor. "We're on aux power now."

We slid the couch in front of the door and collapsed upon it, listening to the screaming from the other side. The siren continued to wail. Tyler pulled me close, holding my head to his chest and covering my exposed ear with his hand. The sounds were now muffled, but that didn't quiet the fact that whatever horror was going on outside was still there. I focused on the sound of his heartbeat. He started talking.

"Say that again," I asked, pulling his hand away from my ear. The loudness of the gruesome sounds returned.

"We'll stay here until things quiet down, then go out and see what's going on."

"Why don't we go now? What if someone needs help?" My voice didn't sound convincing even to me. I didn't know if I was being brave or dumb.

"Are you serious? Don't you hear what's going on—" Something slammed against the door so hard that the couch jolted. However, the impact proved that even though we were on auxiliary power, the door's automatic lock did in fact still work. Hopefully, it would still function properly when we wanted to get out.

A guttural moan came from the other side of the door, then a halfhearted scream. The siren suddenly stopped. For a moment, all I could hear was our breathing as we clung to each other for comfort.

Then the sounds of tearing and cracking and slurping started. We leaned toward the door, nearly putting our ears against it. Further away down the hall, more screaming continued, but there was something right outside my door—right up against it.

We said nothing to each other and sat there for what felt like hours, listening.

Finally, when it was silent, when whatever was making noise outside my door stopped, Tyler leaned into me and whispered, "Let's go out and see what's going on."

I trembled. There was no way I was going out there.

"Come on, Annie. We have to see what happened. And I'll need to help the crew get the main power back on."

I shivered again, and he pushed me off the couch. I once more recoiled at the cold floor and climbed back up. With my knees to my chest, I rocked back and forth on the seat cushion. Tyler moved about my living unit; I was aware of that at least but couldn't focus on what he was doing. In my state of shock, Tyler began to dress me in my maintenance overalls and footwear.

"Let's quietly move this." His voice snapped me back to reality.

Still shivering, I nodded and helped lift the couch out of the way. He put his hand on the door panel. It wouldn't unlock. Panic rose like a hot knife in my chest as though I were about to split open. Tyler held up his index finger, indicating for me to give him a moment. He got a tool and some other things out of my closet and popped open the service panel. I couldn't see what he was doing, but there was a little zap of electricity then a click. The door unlocked. He separated two wires, capped them, and left them exposed. Tyler's a genius with electricity, which is the reason he's in the electrical mechanic unit while I'm in hydro. He's electricity and I'm water. We go so well together.

"I'll have to do that again to lock the door." He held up his finger once more. "Hold on a sec." He got a large butcher knife from the kitchenette drawer—the only weapon I owned. Returning to my side, he grabbed my hand. "Stay close and keep silent."

Tyler pulled open the door.

———

Present Day . . . 14 hours remaining

Dr. Miriam said that it took twenty-four hours for the infestation to reach its full effect before the host died and turned into a mindless eating machine. Tyler cannot be near me after I die. The twenty-four hours allows me one last night with him under my synthetic down quilt on my full-size bed, barely large enough for the both of us. I'll leave early in the morning, before the infestation fully takes over my body.

"I'm going to heat these up," I say, grabbing two meat and two pasta puree packets then hobbling over to the kitchenette. My leg went numb a few minutes ago; I know the normal sensations will never return, but I still have time.

"Maybe you should sit down, put something on that knee," Tyler says.

I wave him off, turning my attention to our improvised stove made from a Bunsen burner taken from the lab and a small pot. Using electricity for the microwave is out of the question. We must conserve every precious watt until help arrives . . . if help is even on its way. One of the caveats in taking on this mission was we were on our own, out in the furthest reaches of the solar system.

I hear Tyler checking the tape we put over each vent, ensuring that all are still sealed. I know the stuffiness of my living unit is getting to him when he peels off the plastic layers covering the largest vent by the bed and quickly tapes on a screen wrapped in nylon fabric against the vent's faceplate. It's rare for him to expose a vent like that, but it's becoming stuffier in here as each day passes.

"There's barely any air coming through." He stands with his face nearly plastered against the screen.

On auxiliary power, nothing runs at full speed. And I'm sure the air handlers haven't been scrubbed since the infestation. The odds are high that there's no one left to maintain them. Tyler and I certainly can't. It's not our specialty. Each maintenance crew member aboard this station had a specialty, but we aren't cross-trained or as versatile as we should be. Backups and redundancies save lives. Many of us aboard the station are too specialized to be able to maintain full life support.

As the food heats, he continues his dinnertime routine of checking every crack and crevice to the outside, which we sealed up in some form or fashion.

Yet, through all the caution and protection, we couldn't keep them out. One got in. It must've happened when he went out this morning, dressed in the spacewalk suit, to forage for food. We're always so careful about opening the doors. Whoever stays behind watches and listens for them.

This morning I sat on the sofa, reading a book and waiting for Tyler to return when I heard a buzzing sound. My throat tightened. The buzzing was all over the room; I couldn't pinpoint it. No matter how hard I tried, I couldn't find the intruder.

———

Almost Three Months Ago . . . 2,189 hours remaining

Paul, Tyler's best friend, knelt over someone toward the end of the corridor. Whoever it was, they were injured, and Paul looked to be trying to help them. A long streak of blood on the floor led from my door to them. Tyler placed a hand on my shoulder, stopping me from taking another step. The look on his face told me to wait.

As he took long, stealthy steps toward Paul, I followed, slowly moving forward. Something wasn't right. The corridor was in disarray, with dropped paperwork, tool kits, and other oddities that workers carried back and forth between jobsites. On the floor, a few feet before me, lay a pipe. Tyler had a knife on him, so I should be carrying something too, right? He might not always be able to protect me. The cold pipe felt heavy and firm in my hand.

"Auugh!" Tyler screamed.

Paul had him pinned on his back to the ground. Tyler's knee was to Paul's chest, keeping him from sinking his gnashing teeth into Tyler's face. Blood coated Paul's arms, face, and chest. Before I knew what I was doing, I was upon them, swinging the pipe and connecting hard with Paul's head. He made a wet groaning sound as he fell to his side. Tyler rolled with his friend, now on top of Paul and about to slam the butcher knife into Paul's chest.

"Ty—" I reached out to him, but it was too late.

He buried the blade to the hilt in his friend's chest. Blood gushed from Paul's mouth, eyes, and nose. Tyler jumped off his body and stumbled over to me. Paul's blood covered his maintenance jumpsuit.

"I didn't mean to—" he choked and pointed to the body on the floor that Paul had been hunkered over. It was a woman, but we couldn't tell who without getting close enough to look at her name tag. Her face was cracked open, like an egg, and the soft tissue of her head scooped out.

———

We found Dr. Miriam hiding in her dark lab. Pushing the doors open, we heard the sound of tape ripping.

"Get out of here!" She ran at us with a metal tray.

Tyler pushed me to the side. The tray hit him in the shoulder. Before she could draw it back, he yanked it away.

"Oh, you're alive." Whatever fiery passion had made her want to kill us fizzled out, and she returned to her monotone self. Then she turned her attention to the door, slamming it shut and smoothing the wide Mylar tape back into place.

"What the hell?" Tyler yelled, throwing the tray to the floor.

"QUIET!" she whispered harshly.

That is when I noticed all her windows were covered and taped in paper, even the ones on the door. And all the seams around the door were taped. Looking around the lab, I saw the vents were also covered.

"What's going on?" I whispered to her.

"Our demise." She shrugged and walked over to the wall of terrariums. The one that once housed the brilliantly colored flies was shattered. The other ones looked normal, except that all the insects inside were dead, covered with a thin white powdery film.

"I killed these with insecticide," she said, placing her hand on one of the intact tanks. "I killed them all to try to save us. To save us from there being more."

Tyler grabbed her upper arm and spun her around. "Save us from what?"

"From my babies."

Her babies? Then I remembered the conversation I'd had with her while fixing the lab's sink. "The pretty rainbow-colored flies?"

"Yes."

Aghast, Tyler said, "Lady, you're nuts. Flies don't cause . . . They don't cause whatever the hell is going on around here."

"What's going on is a newly identified species."

"Newly identified?" I asked, unsure if I wanted the answer.

A dark smile spread across her face. Her eyes sparkled as she spoke. "I found something. Technically, NASA found it, and I commandeered it for Thenurgee."

"You stole something from NASA?" Tyler asked.

"Commandeered," she corrected him. "I was with NASA prior to joining this mission on the *Parallax*. As you know, I'm Earth's leading scientist on genetics and extraterrestrial life."

I rolled my eyes at her declaration of being a world-renowned expert. *Hardly.*

"Thenurgee gave me an offer I couldn't refuse. I brought my work on genetics with me when I joined the space division." She nodded her head to the terrariums that held the now-dead insects. "Remember when you said that genes are not altered in space? You were wrong. The genetics of all those insects—flies aside—were in the process of rewriting themselves. Quite a remarkable finding, despite working under the guise that my job aboard this station was to study the effects of space and radiation on a human's body."

"You were trying to figure out how long we can live in space before the elements, cosmic rays, or whatever change us into, like, primordial goo?" Tyler said, his voice heavy with disdain and disbelief.

"Something like that." By her tone, she was annoyed, but she had a captive audience. "My theory is correct in that exposure to the environment of space and unprotected radiation over a prolonged period does in fact alter a living being's DNA sequence. Changing them into an entirely new and stronger being." She glared at Tyler. "Not primordial goo."

"But you said you ran the experiments on the other insects, not the flies. Are you doing something different to them?" I asked.

The dark smile spread across her face again. "Those beautiful little flies . . . Well, space doesn't seem to alter their DNA. At least from what I can hypothesize at this point in time."

Tyler and I looked at each other in confusion.

Her smile dimmed as she saw that we weren't understanding. "The flies aren't from Earth."

A cold tingle shot down my spine. *Not from Earth?*

"Wh . . . What?" Tyler stammered.

"What I *commandeered* from NASA was a meteorite that had landed in Alaska. An old dogsled trainer found it on his property. He got in contact with the government, then NASA got involved, and the meteorite was given to me to identify its makeup. I couldn't because the elements of the rock didn't trace to any anything on our periodic table. It's something that isn't from our known galaxy. However, that wasn't the most interesting aspect of the discovery. While scraping samples off the meteorite's surface, I found little bodies hidden within the pitted crevasses of the rock. The carcasses of extraterrestrial life-forms."

She narrowed her eyes at the wall behind Tyler and I. "NASA kept most of my work secret. Anything that did get released to the public went under the name of my department's head scientist instead of me. I kept the carcasses a secret from NASA and reached out to Thenurgee with a proposal. They gave me more than I asked for—free rein. When I got aboard the *Parallax* three years ago, my real work began. I figured out how to reanimate these life-forms."

"You brought creatures—*alien* creatures—back to life?" Tyler said.

She said nothing, but pride and power glinted in her eyes.

"What happened?" I asked, numb to her comment, and nodded toward the shattered terrarium that used to house the colorful flies. I didn't care how she did it. All I cared about was *what* happened and what we could do to keep ourselves safe.

"The commander came in about an hour after you left yesterday. His anger got the best of him when he found out the nature of my *real* research. He tried to stop me. So I freed them. He stood right next to the tank, about to take it. I threw a Bunsen burner at it, shattering the glass. My babies swarmed him, covering his face, and he ran from my lab. They followed him out."

"But what's going on aboard the ship?" Tyler asked. "My friend Paul was eating some lady's face. Then he tried to eat me! I had to . . . I had to kill him."

She swooped her hand toward the intact tanks. "After bringing the flies back to life, I became curious about how they'd interact with the insects from Earth. I placed a single fly in an inhabited tank and observed. It turns out, the flies reproduce via parthenogenesis and are larviparous."

I looked at Tyler. His face was set stone cold.

She sighed. "All the flies are female and carry live larvae within their reproductive system. There were no male life-forms found in the meteorite. In other words, a female can asexually give birth without a male. Each fly that I put into an inhabited tank injected her larvae into one of the insects then immediately died. Within a few hours, the larvae essentially took control of the host's body. The host then ate the other, noninfested insect. The same thing happened in every tank."

"Ate the other insect?" I asked.

"Larvae need nutrition to grow quickly. My theory is that the host will eat whatever protein it can find to nourish the larvae, helping them to grow." She put her finger to her chin and walked around the lab, looking at the ceiling. "Once the larvae transform to adult stage, which seems to happen within twenty-four hours, the adults burrow out of the body—through soft tissue like the eyes or nose. The host is no longer animated once the flies leave." She chuckled.

Tyler narrowed his eyes. "People are eating each other!"

I placed my hand on Tyler's chest. We needed to stay levelheaded to get answers. "How long ago did you bring these flies back to life? Yesterday was the first time I had seen them in the lab."

"The ones you saw were six months old. They were growing in the back room. I only brought this batch out here to begin the experiment with the Earth insects. The average life span of a housefly is about a month. This life-form doesn't seem to die until they've injected their larvae. It's like their larvae are their source of life."

"This batch? You mean you have more of these flies?"

"I have more carcasses that I haven't reanimated."

Tyler's face turned red and through gritted teeth he asked, "How did you bring them back to life?"

Ignoring him she went over to a long table on the other side of the room with an equally long black bag on top and wheeled it over to us. "I had to tape up all the cracks to keep the flies out. And I taped up the windows so the infested didn't see me and break in."

She unzipped the bag. The stench was so overwhelming that I turned and vomited. Dr. Miriam looked at me, disgusted. The commander's body and head were cut open in the bag, his brain exposed.

"I needed to see what happened to the body once infested." Her voice sounded detached and far away. "I caught him after he was bitten and conducted my observations on the larval stages of the flies. It was a messy dissection since I didn't have time to drain the fluids."

———

Present Day . . . twenty-four hours remaining

When the buzzing stopped, I knew I was doomed. My arms contour around myself, swatting and slapping, tossing my hair, shaking my clothes. Anything to make the buzzing start again, because if it's alive, then I'm alive too. As I shake myself all over, praying to God that my mind is playing tricks, I catch sight of a black dot, the size of a nickel, on the floor in front of my shoe.

"Please don't be dead; please don't be dead."

I touch it with my finger. The little fly doesn't stir, remaining on its back with her gross little legs pointing into the air. It's dead. And soon I'll be the same. Picking up the disgusting creature, I run to the sink and drop it down the drain. Water splashes everywhere as I turn on the faucet to wash down the tiny corpse.

In the bathroom, my clothes lay in a pile at my feet as I stand in front of the mirror, naked, inspecting my body for the spot where the fly injected her children into my body. It's a fruitless venture because the injection site is a little red pinprick and painless. The moment the larvae are injected into the skin, they burrow down into the muscle and catch a ride in the bloodstream to the brain. There are no welts or bruises left behind as evidence. Once in the brain, the larvae dig into the gray matter and feast.

That is what happened to Dr. Miriam when we tried to leave her. Tyler opened the door and a fly flew in, landed on her face, and bit. In the next twenty-four hours, we watched her transform and go insane from the larvae burrowing into her brain. We killed her before she could attack us.

The same fate now awaits me.

———

Present Day . . . fourteen hours remaining

"I found the bones of a bird, like a parakeet," Tyler says as he slurps up his pasta packet.

"Probably one of Miriam's test subjects. How could the commander not know what she . . ."—I cough, choking back tears—". . . was doing."

"Yeah, the bird probably saw some shit and had even worse stuff done to it. The bones were picked clean. I'm just happy I didn't run into anyone out there." He holds his packet in his hands and stares at his half-eaten meal. "Annie, I don't know how many are left alive aboard the ship. We may be the last. Just us and the flies. I hope that it's just you and me. I can't take killing people anymore."

I shiver as the thought of Tyler beating me with a pipe shoots through my head. "Let's talk about something happier." I don't want to think about death any longer. I still have time.

Tyler starts reminiscing about sports, football specifically. He loves football and has missed it since we launched nearly five years ago. I try to hang on to his every word but start to feel a little sick to my stomach. I shake my head and collect our dinner's trash; all the while he keeps talking about football.

In a daze, I walk over to the sink. The mostly empty packets fall to the floor; I stare at my hand that just let them drop. My arm straightens, my fingers pinch together to my thumb then open then pinch together again—of their own accord. Tyler looks at me and I laugh, muttering something about butterfingers.

The crunching sound starts when I crouch and, with the hand I still have control over, try to wipe up puree that had oozed from a packet onto the floor. My heart quakes in my chest. The crunching is maddening, reverberating in my head.

"Annie, what are you doing—" He watches me crouched, rocking back and forth on the balls of my feet, puree beneath the soles of my shoes. Tyler walks over, taking tentative steps. He loops an arm under my armpit and tries to help me stand. My body doesn't cooperate. Twenty-four hours, a lie. I'm nearly out of time.

—

Present Day . . . ~~fourteen hours remaining~~
five minutes remaining

I fall out of his grasp, crumpling to the floor. Tyler brings his hand up to my neck, palpating the skin for a heartbeat. The moment I fall, the quaking in my chest ceases.

"You're infested!" He runs over to the spacewalk suit and nearly tears through a leg as he tries to pull it on. "Sorry, Annie."

I'm sure he is remorseful, but his voice comes out panic-stricken as he speaks to my clinically dead body. All the while I lay there, my mind still conscious, watching him. I'm dead yet, at the same time, still alive.

I will Tyler to move faster, to run away from here, to get away from me.

—

Present Day . . . one minute remaining

The first jerky movement makes me want to scream, if I could still control my mouth. Tyler, fully suited, pushes the sofa out of the way and tries to override the door locks.

———

Almost Three Months Ago . . . 2,184 hours remaining

The larvae of the *Apocephalus miriamus*—which is what she named her babies—must continually take on nutrients to grow.

"The host must constantly eat to provide that nutrition. To conserve energy and focus all nutrients to the brain for the larvae. I—" She coughed up blood. I moved forward to help, but Tyler held me back. She continued, "I believe the larvae shut down most of the body's functions—lungs, heart, liver, kidneys, 50 percent of the nervous system—leaving just the brain, muscles, and digestive system active."

She concocted her theory with her dying breath that once the larvae hatch and start eating the brain, they emit electrical pulses that override the human driver of a body. The electrical pulses not only take control of the brain but also stimulate the muscles to move the body.

"Those who succumb to the larvae are clinically dead; their body becomes a puppet. Being confined to the space station, the only food for a reanimated human to catch is another human."

Miriam had truly brought to life a monster the size of a nickel. She was successful in achieving her true mission but left behind a legacy that still swarmed the corridors. The more flies that hatched, the more of the *Parallax* crew died.

"I am God" were her last words as her children ate her brain.

We hadn't recorded her theory for her because one moment she was speaking to us, the next she was coming at us. I bashed her head open with my pipe, and we ground her brains under our shoes to kill the larvae before they reached their adult form.

———

Present Day . . . zero minutes remaining

"Fucking MOVE!" He isn't able to override the door. My arms and legs figure out how to work without my control and pull my body upright. I feel nothing, but my eyes lock on him. As a prisoner in my head, I watch myself advance on him. He grabs my pipe that leans next to the door and, without hesitation, bludgeons me. A sharp crack echoes as metal connects with my skull, but I feel nothing. My body stumbles, yet even with my right eye now gone blind, my body still moves toward him.

I beg my body to stop, to hold back, to spare him. I try to bargain with the larvae in my brain. They don't listen.

"Annie, stay away."

The pipe strikes me in the chest. When it cracks my sternum, my hands grab it, wrenching the weapon from him. Inside of his space-walk helmet, Tyler's eyes are wide. Tears sparkle, illuminating the brownish-amber tint of his irises that I love so much.

Even if I could break through and stop my body from attacking, it's only a matter of time before someone else catches him or he's bitten by a fly. I can't let that happen to him—to be killed by something unfamiliar. It's best if I'm the one that helps him leave this world. At least one of us will be immediately free. I'll stay trapped here until the flies burrow out of my head. Then I'll be free too.

We can be together again.

Yes, it's better if things happen this way.

We're out of time.

Where The Elk Roam

"People are Strange" echoed off the outer walls of the empty buildings. The Doors song, stuck on repeat, transmitted haunting lyrics far past the resort, through the valley, and into the mountains. That should've been their sign to leave. Sara couldn't stand another second of this torture. "Do you know how to turn this music off?"

Dags ignored her. She scratched nervously at her arm and looked around. This song had always disturbed Sara. Every time she heard it, she felt as though she were going to be kidnapped by a group of deranged people who looked like they had fallen out of an Edward Gorey drawing.

"Hey, I know we're here to bag your big trophy and that you only brought me along to mind the camp. But, *please* . . ." The looped song began to drive her mad as they unpacked the truck. *Someone must've forgotten to turn the music off when everyone vacated,* she thought. However, she found that quite hard to fathom, given it was just this one song playing on repeat. *Leaving on the music had to be intentional. Maybe to scare the elk away from the center of the resort . . . or to scare away poachers, like Dags.*

After the truck was unloaded and all their gear laid in a heap upon the ground, Dags opened the driver's side door.

"What are you doing?" Sara asked.

"Moving the truck to the far lot so that if anyone gets past the main gate's barriers, they won't see it. Don't want anyone finding us here."

Sara shook her head. "No one's going to come. Everybody knows the resort is closed. Dags, please. The music."

He grumbled and slammed the door shut hard, making Sara jump. She was on edge, and not only because of the music.

It was illegal to be at the resort this time of year. Like clockwork, between September and October, a herd of elk—nearly 2,500— migrated from the forest, through this resort, and continued to the town of Estes Park. The game commission shut down the resort when the herd moved through due to the danger to humans. Elk during rut could go on a murderous rampage.

While the hunting season in the surrounding area outside of the migratory path was open, Dags would be in double trouble if caught, as here they were on private property. Plus, rifle season didn't start until next month, and a rifle was the only firearm he'd brought along. Dags couldn't be bothered with a muzzleloader or archery. Too much work. A rifle was simpler.

"Let's turn that shit off," Dags said.

"I bet we could turn it off from in there." Sara pointed toward the ski resort lodge.

"Like that would be open."

"Never hurts to try." She brushed past him and walked toward the rustic two-story lodge. All the buildings in the resort felt oddly out of place among the Rockies. A Nordic essence inspired the heart of the resort's design, possibly to lure those bored with the Colorado log cabin–esque design. While the design stuck out culturally, the color palette complemented the surrounding forest. If it wasn't for the stripped land around the resort that led up the mountain for the ski routes, one would struggle to see the resort buildings and vacation homes hidden among the trees.

As they ascended the steps to the massive deck of the lodge, an icy blast from the east cut them to the bone.

"Thought it would be warmer today," Dags grumbled.

Sara tightened her jacket at the throat. Off to the right, toward the mountain, in the direction of where the elk would descend, the breeze intensified and ruffled her short black hair. Something large stood at the base of the mountain just at the outer edge of the closest ski slope. Sara raised a hand to her eyes and squinted into the wind, trying to get a better look at what was out there. "Do you see that?"

Dags didn't even look, just pushed past her up the stairs. Heat rose behind Sara's eyes as she glared at him before returning her attention to ski slope. Whatever was out there had disappeared.

"Guess you were right . . . for once." Dags pulled on the heavy handle of the wooden door. It swung open, hinges creaking as they walked in. The lobby sat in the center of the two-story entryway, housing the registration desk. Off to the left, a massive stone fireplace served as a focal point to a lodge room with supple brown leather couches strategically placed about. To the right was a little coffee shop; next to that, a grand staircase with a tree-inspired wrought-iron railing wrapped partially around the lobby and up to the second floor.

They took the stairs, disregarding the "Employees Only" sign, to what seemed to be the administrative floor. Every door stood wide open. Curiosity enticed them to investigate each room and see if they could find anything that resembled audiovisual equipment. At the end of the hallway, they discovered the security room with its door closed.

"Well, looky here," Dags said as he opened the door. One would expect the room to be humming with electricity and monitors displaying live video feeds of the resort's property, but the security room stood dead.

"At least we won't get caught," said Sara.

Dags shrugged. "Even if they had all this running, Eric would have handled it for us."

Eric was Dags's best friend and the area's game warden. He was the only person who knew they were at the resort. Eric had helped Dags plan this little excursion and then looked the other way. Sara didn't believe Eric held any power to aid them should they be caught trespassing, but she held her tongue as her eyes fell on another door to the left of the main security console, also closed. A green light shone on a keycard reader attached to the wall next to the door frame, indicating that it was unlocked. Dags pulled the door open with ease, revealing the server room for the whole resort.

"Weird they left all this unlocked," Sara said.

"Who cares. There's the sound system." He pointed to a rack that held a massive stereo receiver full of knobs, buttons, and switches. In the entire technology-filled room, the receiver was the only thing running. Not even the servers whirled. The panel went black when Dags pushed the blue power button at the top left of the receiver. "Let's go see if that took care of the damn music."

They walked into the hallway. Dags started toward the stairs, but curiosity pulled Sara's attention to closed doors at the other end of the hall.

"Wait. I want to see what's there."

"No, let's go. We need to get camp set up before dark."

"It's only noon. We have a few hours of daylight. This won't take long."

He followed her toward two wooden doors that stood tall from floor to ceiling.

"Wonder what they keep in there. Godzilla?" He laughed while Sara admired the hand-carved scene that adorned every inch of the doors, depicting the Colorado mountains with several elk herds wandering through the valleys.

Sara fingered an oddly carved symbol lightly etched on the side of a mountain. Three-pronged and curled, the symbol was reminiscent of a Celtic triskele. Compared to the craftsmanship done on the rest of the panels, this looked like a toddler had carved asymmetrical, unclean lines.

"Here's another one." Dags pointed to one hiding underneath an elk. As they peered at the carving, they discovered more and more symbols.

Sara ran an index finger over another one, delicately tracing the symbol's design. "What does it mean?"

"Who cares?" Dags shrugged then pushed the doors open.

The darkness inside consumed them, and for a moment Sara thought she'd fallen into a pit. The atmosphere sat heavily on her shoulders as she proceeded blindly toward a thin crack of light emanating from the opposite wall. She waved her hands in front of herself at thigh height to ensure she didn't bump into any furniture.

As she threw open the curtains, dust motes littered the sharp beam of light that cut through the darkness of the office. Sara coughed as the overhead lights flicked on. Dags had found the switch.

The illuminated opulence of the office had a European vibe. Sara assumed the resort was established from old money brought over to America from across the pond and that the owner must've been of Nordic ancestry.

On the wall surrounding the fireplace, heads of various wildlife hung, their glass-eyed, vacant stares looking nowhere and everywhere. A shiver ran through Sara at the sheer number of stuffed carcasses that overwhelmed the room.

Full mounts of smaller animals sat in suspended animation on the fireplace hearth. Sara counted a bobcat, two pheasants, and a few weasels. In the corner next to her, a large black bear reared tall on its hind legs. The most peculiar mount, however, was the fat orange tabby cat on the resort owner's desk, which faced a large leather executive chair that Dags now occupied with his feet propped up on the desk. Hands behind his head, he sighed. "Pretty wicked in here. Can you see me ruling this place?"

"More like running it into the ground."

He laughed. "Oh, like you're so great. Can we go set up camp now?"

She rolled her eyes. "Yeah."

He stood and walked toward the exit. As Sara followed, she noticed the edge of a second doorframe behind one of the office doors.

"Hang on." She pulled the main door back to reveal a shorter one that stood just a bit taller than Dags. The door, painted black, had a larger carved symbol—the misshapen triskele—painted with gold sparkles.

"BDSM closet?" Dags laughed.

Sara glared at him then grabbed the brass doorknob. Locked; the only door locked in the whole place.

"Totally someone's sex dungeon," Dags said.

"Knock it off," Sara said as she pushed past him, leaving the office.

———

They set up camp on top of a small hill outside the resort with a clear view of the surrounding area.

"Prime location. Definitely bagging the one with the biggest rack." Dags loaded his rifle with a magazine cartridge and chambered a round.

"They aren't here yet." While Sara didn't necessarily hate guns, she sometimes didn't trust whoever operated the firearm. She especially didn't like having a loaded gun around when it didn't need to be.

"But I'll be ready when they come." He raised the scope to his eye, sighted into the resort, and hummed with satisfaction.

While he played sniper-atop-the-hill, Sara distracted herself by setting up camp and building a small firepit to cook dinner. She knew Dags wouldn't move from his spot until the food was ready; even then, she'd probably have to bring it to him.

"I'm getting firewood," she said.

Dags didn't move to help or even acknowledge her.

———

Sara would have to make a few trips. First to gather kindling and then another trip to bring back a fallen tree or large branches that could be cut up with the axe.

The forest trees stood tall, dwarfing her against the foothill grasslands. A mix of aspen, beech, and evergreen trees—the perfect candle scent could be based on this exact location. As the sun began to set, the temperature dropped. Goosebumps electrified Sara's skin, elicited by a cold fear that raked through her body as she looked into the dark forest. She hesitated, not wanting to step foot beyond the tree line, yet at the same time an invisible thread tugged at her chest, as though the forest wanted to reel her in. A movement off to her right broke the trance.

Fifty yards away stood the biggest animal she'd ever seen. As a rather tall woman of nearly six feet, had she been standing next to the elk, her head would have barely cleared his shoulder. The elk's antlers were thick and gnarled like the branches of an old oak tree. They looked nearly impossible to hold up. Soft strings of sphagnum moss hung from the tines, giving him a gossamer appearance. He looked ancient, yet thick muscles and sinew rippled under his fur with each slight movement. However, for Sara, the most captivating trait of this beast was a stark white streak that started at his coal-black nose and traced up between his eyes and antlers. The streak stood out in contrast to the ruddy color of the rest of the elk's body. She assumed that it continued down his neck and back but couldn't be sure of that from her vantage point. The streak stood out, imparting an almost-glowing stripe through his tattered brown fur.

The elk snorted. The ground beneath Sara's feet seemed to tremble. She looked down to where his hooves met the grass and grimaced; fear quivered in her heart at the sight of them, nearly the same size as a Clydesdale horse's. If she provoked him in any way, she'd be trampled and killed instantly. Sara backed away in the direction of the camp, never taking her eyes off him.

The elk snorted once more and bobbed his head while stomping a hoof. Black eyes glinted with a mix of what looked like anger and curiosity. She continued to back away. He never moved but kept his eyes fixed on her. When Sara felt as though she'd put a sufficient distance between herself and the elk, she turned and sprinted back to camp. At one point she looked back to be sure he still stood at the tree line, but he'd disappeared, as though the forest had absorbed him.

"Dags!" she called out as she ran into camp. "I just saw the biggest elk ever." Sara stretched her arms out as wide as possible with the tips of her fingers pointed to the sky. "The rack had to be at least this big."

"Give me a break. That's like over six feet. No elk has a rack that big."

"Dags, I'm serious! You need to look for him. The rack was thick, like a heavy tree branch. And old. And—"

"Enough! Did you get the firewood? I'm hungry."

"But—"

"You embellish everything. You've never seen an elk, so how do you know how big they really are?"

Sara shut her mouth and turned away. Tears pricked at the corner of her eyes.

The sun descended behind the mountain ridge while they bickered. "I'm not going into the forest now that it's getting dark." She knew he'd never agree to go with her. "Guess we're having granola bars and PB&J sandwiches for dinner."

"Oh, for fuck's sake, Sara!"

———

She shivered inside her sleeping bag. Dags hated having anything against him while he slept and wouldn't allow her to curl up next to him for warmth. Once again, Sara found herself wondering why she stayed with him. Her friends told her that he didn't bring any purpose to her life. In fact, being with him hindered her from obtaining her dreams.

Sara wanted to achieve a level of success and greatness in her life that would make her father proud. She had wanted to move to the East Coast to study astronomy and astrophysics at Villanova University. With that kind of education, she'd be able to make breakthrough discoveries that she could bring to the world, such as finding a new planet that humanity could inhabit.

Through the small plastic window on the roof of the tent, she stared at the night constellations, finding Taurus painted in the sky. Her father once joked as they lay on a blanket in the field next to her childhood home that stargazers must never look at the red eye of the bull—the star Aldebaran—as gazing upon it would drive a person mad.

"But, Dad, you always tell me I'm crazy with my head out in space." She laughed.

He splayed his fingers and grasped her face as he whispered, "We're all mad here."

"Dad!" Sara had pushed his hand away and smiled at the man she most admired in life. An accomplished NASA astrophysicist, he had left a prestigious job in Washington, DC, to move to Colorado, where he took on work as an astronomy professor for a community college. Sara never found out why her father had made that move, but she believed it was for the clearer Colorado night skies.

"Your craziness will push you to take risks and discover new worlds. All scientists have a little madness in them." Those were some of the last words he'd ever say to her. Two days later, he was a victim of a fatal car accident.

Her father was the only person who supported her dreams of space. When he died, her hope of achieving greatness died too. No one in her family understood her determination to be like her father. They thought her too fanciful and said she should focus on something more grounded, such as a business career that would make her money. Her family saw no value in looking at the stars.

Sara had felt lost until she met Dags when they were seventeen. At first he fed into her fascination with the night sky, encouraging her to teach him the constellations and how to navigate by the stars. But once the newness of the relationship wore off, Dags turned his attention back to his own interests of hunting and working on his truck. Their late romantic nights in the field to stargaze and make love had ceased. Sara wanted to believe it was because the nights were turning cooler, but when summer rolled around, there was still no stargazing. And there hadn't been for the past four years.

But Dags was stability. She knew what she was getting with him, knew her future. At times she yearned to pack up her life and try to get into the Villanova undergraduate program, despite graduating high school almost six years ago with average grades. She'd have to go it alone. Dags had no intention of leaving Colorado. Born and bred in these mountains, his whole lineage existed here on the land around Estes Park.

As she stared into the red eye of Taurus, Sara knew she'd never achieve anything beyond becoming Dags's wife. She'd chosen stability over risk; a man over her dreams. Her father was wrong. She wasn't a scientist. A scientist would be mad enough to gamble the risk of striking out on their own to achieve their life goals.

———

Dags woke Sara just before the sun peeked above the ridge. When he left the tent, Sara rolled over to absorb the body heat left behind in his sleeping bag. Once his warmth disappeared, she quickly changed her clothes and crawled out of the tent to find him already in his spot, observing the surrounding area through his rifle's scope.

"They're here," he whispered. Sara pulled his binoculars out of his pack, wrapped herself up in a blanket, and sat down next to him. She couldn't clearly see individual elk, as the sun's morning rays hadn't fully surmounted the mountain ridge. For the moment, the migration looked like a black mass of movement undulating from the edge of the forest, down the fields, and into the valley surrounding the resort. A sea of bodies ebbed and flowed around the buildings.

"Can you see one?"

"There's like a thousand of them," Dags said. He took the binoculars from her. She opened her mouth to protest because he could keep using his rifle scope to scout, but his glare indicated she would cross the line if she said anything. "This is going to be impossible to find the biggest."

"Maybe that old one will show up. I could help you look for him if I had those binoculars and you used your scope."

"Be quiet." He reached up and clamped a hand over her mouth, the binoculars steady in his other hand. Sara wrenched her head away, irritated that he'd grabbed her face, and returned her gaze to the distant herd in front of them.

———

They sat there for a few hours, eating granola bars and drinking water, looking out across the valley. The temperature warmed to where Sara spread the blanket on the ground; she lay upon it on her stomach to observe the area around the resort. For reasons she couldn't explain, she felt exposed on the hill as though something watched her from beyond the trees.

They hadn't spoken since he'd told her to stop talking. For someone who hated silence, he demanded it while hunting. Sara thought about counting the elk to see how many were in the herd, but there were many clusters so tightly packed that she struggled to differentiate individuals. Her attention drifted to a part of the herd that milled around the edge of the forest to the right of where they sat.

Those elk acted differently.

"Can I have the binoculars? I'd like to see something."

He ignored her.

"Dags," she said a little louder, knowing that would annoy him. He shushed her with a glare, then handed over the binoculars.

"Hold these while I go take a piss." He stood and wandered off behind the tent. Sara raised the binoculars to her eyes. The separate cluster by the trees looked agitated. Their heads bobbed, swaying their antlers in what seemed to be a defensive dance. From their noses, hot exhalations puffed in small clouds.

Within an instant, they stilled and then backed away from the tree line. From out of the forest stepped the old elk Sara had encountered the previous evening.

"Dags, Dags!" she whispered as loudly as she could.

As Dags walked up next to her, he grumbled about making too much noise. He picked up his rifle and sat down. As he did, she shoved the binoculars back at him.

"There. Look there. It's him." She pointed and he raised the binoculars, looking in the direction she indicated.

"What the fuck is—"

"See, I told you!"

Dags gasped. "That's not an elk. There's no way."

"What would it be then?"

"Sara, it's huge! It's towering over all the other elk. The antlers are like a moose. Maybe it's, like, a moose-elk hybrid? He's rare."

"He's majestic."

"He's mine." Dags set down the binoculars.

"What? No!" She grabbed his arm as he raised the rifle. "You can't kill him. He's rare. You just said so."

"Are you kidding me?" He pulled his arm away. "Do you know how much money we could make off that rack?"

Sara sat up, grabbed the binoculars, and looked at the old elk, her heart heavy, knowing she'd damned him. She never should've told Dags, though Dags would eventually have spotted him. If only she had kept her mouth shut.

As the old elk walked down toward the resort, the herd parted, the others moving away as though he were plagued. He continued through the common center and exited their side of the resort, well within range for Dags.

Sara couldn't take her eyes off the old elk. He bent his head to the ground to nibble on grass, and Sara clearly saw that the stripe from his nose that continued over his head did in fact travel down his back, only to stop midway and twist into an odd pattern. Sara dropped the binoculars and rubbed her eyes. It couldn't be. She raised them once more to her eyes and registered a familiar symbol formed by the white of his fur.

The same symbol carved on the doors of the resort owner's office.

The elk lifted his head and looked right at her, chewing and swallowing a last bit of grass. His eyes beckoned her, and once more an invisible thread tugged at her chest, a feeling of being pulled toward him.

Sara jolted at the concussion from the rifle, but the binoculars never came away from her eyes. The bullet pierced through the old elk's neck. He staggered, his front knees buckling beneath him. The other elk backed further away. He righted himself and stood tall, returning his intense gaze at Sara. A hot sensation of a sickening dread swelled in her chest. Killing this elk felt like a very bad idea.

Sara, numb to the sound of the second shot, watched as the bullet sought purchase right between those coal-black eyes. The old elk's head dropped. An odd-colored mucus splattered from the back of his skull, and he collapsed to his right side. He didn't even twitch. An instant kill.

All the elk in the valley looked toward where the old elk had fallen, then dispersed, scattering back into the surrounding mountain forests, away from Estes Park.

"Dags, I think we have a problem." The migration was running away. People would notice if this herd didn't begin to trickle into town later in the day and would come looking for them. Fear spread throughout Sara's body. All she wanted to do was tear down camp, pack up the truck, and drive away.

A fleeting feeling pulsed in her mind that those who would come looking for the lost herd would be the least of their worries. Dags seemed to have a similar idea—he had already stood and was packing up his gear. She shook her head to clear the strange feeling, grabbed her blanket, quickly collected the camping items, and dismantled the tent. Every few moments she looked toward where the old elk lay. The sensation of something bad looming made her hurry even more.

Carrying the camping and hunting gear, they trekked down the hill. Sara set her sights on the truck and kept her eyes locked on it as they descended. She didn't want to see the elk again. After several minutes of walking, she didn't feel Dags's presence. When she turned to look for him, she saw him at the elk's carcass. She should have known better. He needed his prize, and the risk of getting caught, or worse, was worth those antlers.

Her nerves rattled as she begrudgingly walked over to him. He had his hunting pack open on the ground with his hands inside, rooting around for something. As Sara neared the elk, his pungent scent caught on the breeze and smacked her in the face: gamey, woodsy, and decaying. The old elk was already dying before Dags had shot him. Dags had just helped him along the journey to death.

"Dags, look." She pointed to the grass where a sickly, green-tinged yellow fluid haloed the elk's head. There wasn't any blood, just the thick mucus-colored ooze.

Dags put down his bag and stood next to Sara, looking at the pattern of liquid that formed before them.

"That's . . . that's the same symbol as the ones on the office door." Sara's voice trembled. "And look, there on his back—the symbol."

"Sara, I don't see anything. It's just a diseased old elk with patches of gray fur. There is nothing supernatural or out of the ordinary here aside from the size of this rack." There was a quiver in Dag's voice that betrayed his fear.

She stepped closer to the carcass, careful to not step in the liquid that spread across the dry grass. The greenish-yellow ooze continued to seep from both bullet holes. Dags reverted to his indifferent state, outwardly neutralizing any evidence of fear.

"Let's cut this rack and get out of here. That meat is diseased." Dags removed a Sawzall and skinning knife from his bag. He approached the elk and carefully stepped around the putrid ooze. With the Sawzall resting on the elk's shoulder, Dags took the tip of his skinning knife and nicked a hole in the scalp before hooking the skin with the sharp side. Sara looked away and focused on the resort. Her thoughts were drawn toward the registration building and the locked door inside the office. In distracting herself from what was going on behind her, she found that she couldn't get that locked door and its sparkly gold symbol out of her mind.

"Sara!"

She turned to see Dags with the skin of the scalp peeled apart, exposing the space on the antlers between the skull and the burr, his Sawzall blade already buried in that space. With one hand on the tool and the other above his head holding the antlers, he glared at her.

"Get over here and hold this," he seethed through his teeth. Anger flashed in his eyes, and Sara tamped down the thoughts of that door as she walked over to help hold the antler, careful not to step in any of the ooze.

A thick, limp purple tongue hung from the elk's mouth. His eyes were glassy and vacant, just like all those mounts in the resort owner's office. A wave of nausea hit her as she thought about the elk's head hanging on the wall above the shorter locked door. She breathed through her mouth as her hands grasped his bone-dry antler. She expected the antler to be gritty and dirty, but it was clean and smooth. Only the strings of moss that hung from the tines marred the antlers' perfection.

Dags turned on the Sawzall again, and the intense motion of the cutting blade vibrated the antler in her hands. When he cut through the full length of space below the burr, the weight of the antler pitched her backward to the ground. She landed on her back, right in the elk's ooze. Her head was the last point to make contact. The antler crashed heavily upon her, a long sharp tine narrowly missing her abdomen.

She let out a wail. Wide-eyed, Dags dropped the Sawzall and helped lift the antler off her. Sara's entire body shook with adrenaline from the near impalement and being covered in the elk's diseased liquid.

"Please, I want to go home." Her voice quivered in concert with the trembling of her hands.

"Eh, sorry. We just need to get this other antler down." Dags set the fallen antler aside and moved toward the other one, not once checking to see if she was okay or bothering to help her up.

Sara felt hot as she lay on the ooze-covered grass, then the quaking of her body ceased. She went stone still.

"No." Her voice sounded distant, hollow, yet firm. The sensation of her back and hair coated in the sticky liquid doused all emotion within her. She felt nothing.

Dags ignored her and put the Sawzall to the second antler. "Hold this one while I cut it."

A fire sparked in Sara's belly, and a slow, burning rage flowed through her. "Take me home now; you can come back here and deal with this on your own."

Maybe it was the flat sound of her voice, or maybe the fire in her belly reached her eyes and he saw the inferno within her. Dags took a step back and set down the Sawzall.

Without a word, Sara turned and walked toward the truck. She heard nothing above the pounding of her heart in her ears. The rage had now fully engulfed her to where she thought about returning to Dags, taking his rifle, and shooting him. The thought passed when she arrived at the truck and saw that he had followed her with no gear or trophy in hand—he carried only his rifle, slung across his shoulders. His hands were jammed in his pockets, searching for the truck keys.

Sara waited patiently by the passenger side door for it to unlock. Nothing.

"Dags. Open the fucking door now." Her voice, still level, was full of venom.

"The fob's battery must be dead." His voice trembled.

Good, she thought. *He's scared because he knows I'm furious but remaining calm. He's probably thinking that I'm going to slit his throat in his sleep.*

The sound of the key sliding into the driver's side door, and seeing it open, brought her a slight relief—until she saw his face through the passenger side window as he reached across to open her door. She climbed in and looked at the rifle that sat between them. Sara did her best to will the thought of "what if" away.

"I'll take you home and see if my uncle or Eric can help me get the rest of this stuff." With shaking hands, he put the key into the ignition and turned it. Sara calmly looked at him. She relished the thought that the elk's bodily liquid smeared all over the back of her clothes now stained his cloth seat. He'd just bought this truck six months ago.

The ignition just clicked. He turned the key again, again, and again.

"What's wrong?" Her anger teetered on the edge of explosion.

"The fucking truck won't start." He kept turning the key. "Did you leave the light on when you got the tent?"

Sara felt her mouth move but had no control over the words that passed her lips. She couldn't contain her anger any longer. "I'll kill you if you blame this all on me. Get me the fuck out of here."

Shock contorted Dags's face as he kept turning the key to no avail. "Um . . ." He ran his fingers through his shaggy brown hair. "Let's go to the lodge and see if we can find something to jump the truck."

Sara felt detached from her body as she swung open the passenger side door, got out, and walked toward the registration building. She heard Dags running behind her, breathing heavily.

He's scared. Scared of me. A giggle bubbled in her chest, but she wouldn't let it out. She wanted him to remain in terror.

They were nearly to the stairs when a voice called from behind them: "Dear friends, we are so grateful for your help."

Sara and Dags whirled around to find a group of about fifteen people dressed in black cloaks. The one who spoke stepped forward. A yellow stripe started at the throat of his cloak and traveled to the ground. To the left side of his chest, he clutched a hardback book that looked to be bound in well-worn leather.

"Where the fuck did you come from?" Dags asked.

"We aren't from here, but with your assistance, friends, we were able to arrive here. My name is Paha."

"Our assistance?" Sara felt back in her body again, the rage subsiding.

"Yes. You opened the doorway for us to come here." Paha's smile grew unnaturally large, displaying a mouth full of stained, crooked and jagged teeth. He bowed and pointed in the direction of the old elk's carcass. "My lady, we come to you from Carcosa through the doorway that he unlocked. We've come to revive our King. Please, come with us to help wake him. He would very much like to meet you."

"Dude, I don't know what kind of drugs you're on and don't care about where you came from, but leave us alone." Dags stepped closer to Sara, but she moved toward the man. Just like the feeling with the elk and the forest yesterday, an invisible thread tugged at her chest. Paha handed the book off to a woman with dark hooded eyes and an equally jagged-toothed smile.

"What is that book?" Sara asked, pointing toward the book the woman now had clutched to the left side of her chest.

"Oh, it's nothing for you to be concerned about. It wouldn't do you any good." Paha clasped his hands together and then looked at Dags. "Would you like to read it?"

"I'm warning you. Get the fuck out of here," Dags snarled.

The group started to hum a tune Sara had never heard before as Paha drew a long sharp dagger from the sleeve of his cloak.

"Please, friends," he said to Dags. "We need you to wake our King."

"How?" Sara asked.

Paha raised his dagger and pointed the tip toward Dags. "He will."

Dags grabbed Sara's arm and pulled her up the stairs to the registration building. He crashed through the front doors, dragging her along. She didn't resist. Dags reached for the door as Sara turned to look at the strangers advancing up the stairs after them. All the strangers had the same toothy, unnatural smile plastered on their pale faces.

Dags slammed the door shut. He fumbled around the door handle, looking for a lock, but the lock required a key.

"Dags . . .," Sara said as he took her hand and pulled her up the stairs to the second floor. The disconnected feeling returned and Sara felt as though she were floating, but it was right to have Dags lead her down the hall to the resort owner's office. The large wooden doors still stood wide open, and he pushed her through, slamming them shut behind them. This time there was a latch he was able to lock.

He jumped backward as she heard the front door downstairs crash open.

"We need to find a way out of here." He frantically looked around the room as Sara stood entranced by the small door that Dags had thought concealed a BDSM closet.

It sat wide open.

"In there!" Dags grabbed her hand and she followed with a light step, neither of them questioning why the door now stood open.

Archaic chanting echoed off the walls of the lobby as she heard Dags feeling the walls for a light switch. Sara stepped inside the room after him. The moment she crossed the threshold, the door slammed shut behind her.

"Sara!" Dags screamed. "Open the door."

She didn't move, welcoming the darkness. A loud crash signaled that the strangers had broken open the office door. The chanting's timbre increased as they neared the final door of separation.

With a popping sound, two large hand-painted symbols began to glow on the walls, one on each side of them. The sickly yellow bioluminescent light from the symbols revealed what had been locked away.

Dags frantically looked around. "An altar. This room is a fucking altar."

Before them, on a short dais, stood a skeleton cloaked in a tattered dark yellow robe, its skull bearing a large rack of antlers like the old elk's. Between the antlers sat a yellowing bone crown. The King. The open folds of the robe revealed the full skeleton. The most peculiar part of the King's body was his lower legs and feet. The tibia and fibula were thin, much thinner than a human's, and the bones ended in hooves like an elk's.

Dags pushed Sara away from the door, but before he could touch the knob, it sprang open, revealing the group of strangers. The chanting quieted as the man in the cloak with the yellow stripe stepped into the room. Dags took a step back, bumping into Sara, who stood firm and immobile against him.

"Dear friends, once again we thank you for your help and generosity." Paha took another step forward.

"Get out of my way," Dags seethed through his teeth.

"My brother, Hiisi, with help from the demiurge Ja, have made things quite difficult. Quite difficult indeed. Despite being our King's closest comrade, my brother believed that the King loved his followers more than him. Somehow, Hiisi tricked our King into sneaking alone to this world. Then he tainted our King's doorway, effectively keeping our King from returning to Carcosa and preventing us from finding him." Paha ignored Dags and widened his grin, the corners of his lips now reaching his ears.

"However, your first attack against the doorway broke Hiisi's seal, and I was able to bring myself and some of the King's followers through before your second attack eliminated the doorway. Now we shall start a new kingdom here, since we cannot return to Carcosa. Thanks to your efforts, you have reunited us with our King," Paha held his hand toward Sara, "and provided us with a new Queen."

Dags turned and looked at her. She couldn't help the smile that stretched across her face. The elk's ooze still wet on her back and hair began to expand down her arms, legs, and then around front to her chest, enveloping her in a warm embrace. She became fully covered from her chin to her toes in a golden liquid that shimmered from the glow of the wall's symbols. The liquid tempered, becoming her new skin. Dags stepped away from her. The corner of the unnatural smile on her lips twitched in satisfaction. Sara could hear Dags's heart pounding. Pounding in absolute terror.

"I'm not going to tell you again; get out of my way," Dags said to the group of strangers.

"I cannot allow that. You are in the court of our King, and we need you for one last task. Please wake our Lord."

"Dags, we need your help. Wake our King." Sara said, feeling an over-whelming sense that all was suddenly right in the world, grabbed his hand. Her smile expanded and a giggle erupted from her lips as she admired her sparkly gold hand holding his shaking one. Dags had given her a purpose in life after all.

He struggled against her pull, but he was helpless against her newfound strength. She dragged him to the altar and pushed him down onto his knees. Taking his face between her hands, she forced him to look at the King. Dags stopped resisting the moment his eyes met the skeleton's empty eye sockets.

"Thank you, Dags," Sara whispered, "for everything. You've helped me achieve greatness. I'm a Queen." She tilted his face to look up at her. Only his red-rimmed eyes moved, meeting her intense gaze. Dags's dilated pupils signaled that the time had come. Someone touched her shoulder. She turned to find Paha holding out his dagger. She took it.

"Sara, you are insane," Dags said, his voice hollow.

With one golden hand still holding his face, she drew the dagger across his throat with the other. His body crumpled to the floor as his blood pooled beneath him. Sara ran her hands through his blood then walked to her King. Bowing before the altar, she ran her bloodied palms down the King's tattered robes. The jaw of the skeleton clacked as muscles bubbled out of bone and wove around the skeletal structure.

Sara then returned to Dags and knelt by his head. Placing a hand on his face one last time, she looked him in the eyes as his life force faded and transferred to her Lord.

Sara kissed his cheek and whispered, "Madness and greatness can share the same face.

About the Author

With a love of scary stories and folklore, Amanda Headlee spent her entire life crafting works of dark fiction. She has a fascination with the emotion of fear and believes it is the first emotion humans feel at the moment they are born. She enjoys writing dark fiction that delves into psychology, folklore, and cosmic horror. The fear of humanity's insignificance in the vastness of the universe intrigues her.

———

By day, Amanda is a portfolio manager; by night, she is a wandering wonderer. When she isn't writing or working, she can be found logging insane miles on one of her many bikes, running the wilds of Pennsylvania, or hiking the Appalachian Mountains.

Amanda wrote of monsters and lore in her debut novel, *Till We Become Monsters*. Her macabre short stories appear in several anthologies, including *Midnight from Beyond the Stars, CONSUMED: Tales Inspired by the Wendigo,* and *That Darkened Doorstep.*

Acknowledgments

The tales contained within *Madness and Greatness Can Share the Same Face* took seven years to accumulate. The journey began with "In the Hollow of Smugglers' Notch" in 2016 and ended with "Carrion Eaters." The latter was prompted by the Queen of Cosmic Horror, Mary SanGiovanni, at the Scares that Care writers retreat in April 2023. The prompt: Open the story with a man lying on the road. I enjoyed writing this story and exploring what lengths a father would go to protect his daughter. That story was my healing journey after writing "The Faunling," which, along with "The Voiceless," cause me to question my sanity.

But I digress.

After completing the first draft of "In the Hollow of Smugglers' Notch," I wondered where the Kafka-inspired aliens originated. As I pondered their creation and existence, I began dreaming up a universe for those extraterrestrials and their creators—and their transcendence outside that universe and into other dimensions. Then, on top of that growing nebulous, I considered how the concepts of "Heaven" and "Hell" fit into the equation. I've lost track of the sleepless nights I tossed and turned in bed, bathed in a sweat of existential crisis.

The ideas were so vast and cosmic that every time I tried to grasp hold of them, they would slip through my fingers and into the ether. I couldn't wrangle my thoughts into concrete ideas and bring these creations in my head to life on paper.

Until now . . .

The catalyst was Monaria's Fright Club, where the lessons learned and two-thousand-word exercises produced during the workshops established the foundation that birthed the first iteration of several stories within *Madness and Greatness Can Share the Same Face*. Those baby stories evolved into the grotesque aberrations they are today. And I couldn't be prouder.

All the tales in this collection have links to one another. Some connections are evident in this collection; others will be revealed through future work.

Thank you to Monar Lawrence, creator of Fright Club and my friend. Your writing advice and guidance helped bring my cosmic mythos to life.

———

To my sister, this first step in revealing the universe in my head is for you because we are of the same mind—whether we like to admit that or not. I hope you enjoyed being written as a cannibalistic host to parasites.

To my parents, thank you for your loving support and . . . um . . . sorry about writing more cannibalism stories. At least this time, no grandmas were murdered.

———

To my family at the Mid-Atlantic Dark Fiction Society—thank you for being kindred spirits and confidants in a world that doesn't always understand us "Halloween People."

———

And to Sprout the Horror Pup, you are fur-ever my apocalypse companion.